Earthly Justice

Earthly Justice

by
E. S. Goldman

TriQuarterly Books

Another Chicago Press

1990

Published by TriQuarterly Books/Another Chicago Press,
1990. Distributed by ILPA, Box 816, Oak Park, IL 60303.

This book has been published with the assistance of the
TriQuarterly Council and the Friends of TriQuarterly.
Additional funding has been made by the Illinois Arts
Council and the National Endowment for the Arts.

Library of Congress #90-80995,
Goldman, E. S.
Earthly Justice

ISBN 0-929968-13-1 (cloth)
ISBN 0-929968-14-X (paper)

The following stories first appeared in the publications
indicated: "Way to the Dump," "Dog People," "Yellow
Jackets" and "Earthly Justice," the *Atlantic*; "Lion Wagon,"
Story; "Running Well," *Cimarron Review;* "A Marriage Kind of
Secret," *Beloit Fiction Journal;* "Nelly Fallower's *Streetcar*,"
Missouri Review; "Good Works," *TriQuarterly*. "Way to the
Dump" also appeared in *The Best American Short Stories 1988*.

Cover illustration: Edward Hopper, *Cape Cod Evening*,
National Gallery, Washington, John Hay Whitney Collection.
Reproduced by permission.

Design by Ray Machura

Contents

7   Way to the Dump

25   Clay Carter's Will

42   Dog People

60   Yellow Jackets

78   Earthly Justice

96   "It Is Hard for Thee to Kick—"

113   Lion Wagon

123   Running Well

135   A Marriage Kind of Secret

150   Nelly Fallower's *Streetcar*

171   Gibson #7

186   Good Works

To Virginia

who sees everything first

Way to the Dump

ZUERNER was breaking away from the Boston meeting to come to the Cape, but surely not because of a casual invitation extended in a passing encounter with Elligott a year ago. Two men who disliked each other for no particular reason, the most incurable kind of aversion; something said for want of something better to say; neither he nor Zuerner had expected it to be taken up. Still, Zuerner had telephoned and asked if it would be convenient if he came by.

Was the merger on again? Did they want his stock?

"Stay for lunch," Elligott had said impulsively, and immediately regretted the sign of weakness. He never managed to get the right tone with Zuerner. He hadn't even had the reserve to say, "Let me look at the calendar." Not even, "Let me see if Daisy can make it for lunch."

Elligott moved the slider and stepped out to his terrace. Unlike early settlers' houses that sought buffers between themselves and wind, the house had been a summer shack before the alterations and wanted to be right there on the low bluff above the beach. Its prospect was across the steaming bay toward an awesome pink dawn. On the way out the tide had trapped his skiff in shore grass; returning, it mirrored the forested dune. Some day! Some scene! Elligott felt the exhilaration of a discoverer. He wondered what he'd have to pay to commission this view from the fellow who did the Indian Marsh paintings in Derek's gallery. It would be worth a thousand dollars. Some week in the market—and now a day like this!

He shrugged comfortably in his new Bean sweater; just the

thing for this chill Sunday morning in October. October—so soon. Quarter to six. Dowling would be open in . . . now fourteen minutes.

Nobody on the water. Nobody anywhere. Not a bird. The only sound a ratcheting cricket augmented in Elligott's hearing aid. He turned for the bearing on the slate surface. Fat with good luck the cricket tensed toward cover but the man's foot was too quick. Elligott felt a small startle at the confrontation, not enough to call fear—afraid of a cricket?—but it would have read on an instrument. Perhaps a blood-admonition not to kill easily. He kicked the squash over the edge into the sand, leaving a stain and a twitching leg on the mortar joint. In an impulse of compassion or guilt he stepped out the twitch.

He stood for another moment at the terrace edge, bothered slightly that the new sun-room, in the nature of all new things, had estranged the house from its environment. It had happened before and he knew now that in a few years the rugosa, creeper, poison ivy, catbrier, fox grape, beach plum and innumerable unidentifiable wind- and bird-brought weeds fleeing upward from the salt would blur the margins of the foundation into the land, and the shingle would darken. The house would then come fully into its destiny. It was an extraordinary house.

He thought of a small boat going by and somebody looking up and saying to himself: that's Elligott, a noticeable man. You would trust your widow to Elligott. Perhaps not your wife; look at the bush of hair for a man his age and the athletic way he carries his weight. A house suitable to the commanding view, what you would expect of a man like Elligott.

The hydrangea he had cleverly placed below the terrace so that its massive plates of bloom could be seen from above was at its fullest. The branch he had layered stood erect in full leaf, surely rooted. He had never imagined that gardening would be so pleasurable, and that he had such a hand for it. Farther below, in the narrow courses veining the grassy marsh, blue crabs fed; mostly big this time of year, no chicks; big as mitts swimming to the rotten-meat bag and taking alarm too late to escape the sneaking net.

Wait till Zuerner began to net crabs down there for his lunch. That would get to him all right. That would open up his face! That would balance all accounts.

The rankle at his forced retirement that Elligott frequently waked with before they came to the Cape had been diminishing all year, and this morning it gave way completely to the expectation of how boggling it would be to Zuerner to see, on this best of all possible days, how well he and Daisy lived.

Gone the clubs and restaurants, the church and duty boards where men who knew he had been pushed aside observed him. He had made known that resigning to become a consultant was his idea, but McGlynn, Andrewes, Draveau, Thompson, Zuerner—all of them and their wives—had known that his resume circulated. Everybody had known. In an office without the dignity of a secretary, without identifiable clients, the walls became transparent. He felt himself become transparent. To distance himself from his telephone he had the building agent's girl record that she was Mr. Elligott's office, and if you waited for the tone you could leave a message of any length. After an interval Elligott called back insurance agents he had never before heard of; the *Wall Street Journal* offered a trial subscription; business papers wanted ads for Consultant Service Indexes; somebody wanted his cousin Lewis Elligott.

And one day Daisy had said, "Why don't we fix up the cottage and see what living on the Cape would be like?"

A steadying wife, what a blessing.

From that came days like this. Today he wouldn't mind comparing lives with Andrewes, Zuerner—with McGlynn himself—any of them. Most of all Zuerner.

An emotion of vacancy seeped in him. He felt as he had after eagling the fifth at The Heights Club; triumph and loss, playing alone, nobody to see the two iron drop, nobody to take the burden of telling from him. In the long run it became a not quite convincing story he could slip into a conversation but couldn't *tell*. Zuerner was the man to sign your card. Zuerner's authority would authenticate Elligott's life to Mc-Glynn, Andrewes, all of them at Allegheny Barge & Dredge.

He decided to take the wagon. It hadn't been turned over all week; do the old girl good to have hot oil in her cylinders and valves. He punched the garage-door button and got in while the door complained to the top and the control panel nattered at him to put on his galoshes, comb his hair, brush his teeth, stop squinting. At The Pharmacy the *Times* would be shuffled by six. Dowling's wouldn't be busy yet, he would be able to open the paper on the counter. Be back before Daisy was even up.

The driveway crackled through the allowed disorder of scratch pines and pin oaks, bayberry and blueberry bushes rising from the rust of pine needles. He regretted mildly that for thirty years he had let the native growth have its way when for a few dollars he could have set seedlings of better breeds that by now would have been massive, towering, elegant. You could truck in hand-split shakes for the roof and Andersen windows with instant Colonial mullions and eighteen-dollars-a-square-foot tiles but only God could make a tree. Only time marketed tall white pines. And rhododendrons like Pauley's.

He bobbed along the stony humpedback lane kept up by the Association—PRIVATE 15 MPH PLEASE OBSERVE—then onto the state blacktop that forked at Way To The Dump, taking him toward town by the back road past Pauley's rhododenrons.

Development had not yet made progress here. The small properties were frugally held by owners who fought mortgages every percent of the way and counted on thirty bags of December scallops to help with the fuel bills. The houses had no views. The families used to grow cranberries in adjacent bogs. Cut off by barrier roads, the bogs were reduced to wetlands unbuildable by law and some years away from the kind of owners who could use the interesting tax consequences of a gift to the Conservation Fund. Some of the houses sat behind pickets not recently painted, of a dimension that to the eye was no longer quite replaceable in an age when everything was a fraction of an inch less than advertised.

But here ancestors and young-marrieds had seen thickened hedges prefigured in a few sticks. He slowed while he envied the maturities. Cedars spiked in a grove of pines; lilacs that, come spring, would bear trusses above a man's reach; Pauley's rhododendrons.

Elligott knew Pauley the way he knew a half dozen building tradesmen around town; he had assumed the driver to be the man whose name was on the truck. He had called Pauley once and asked if he would work up a price on a new shower.

I'll stop next week and look at it. You near Haseley?

Elligott explained how easy it was to find his place from Haseley's. It was the last he heard from Pauley. Par for the trades.

Meanwhile, out of courtesy, Elligott waited three weeks, lost all that time before calling another plumber.

In June the rhododendrons between the road and Pauley's house had been amazing. It was a jungle in there, maybe the bogland accounted for it. Purples, whites, reds, creams shot with yellow, ink and blood spatters. Like a park. There must be fifty or sixty plants in there, some of them giraffe-high, twenty or forty thousand dollars' worth if you had to truck them in that size and set them, and all from a few sticks. Imagining the plumber's rhododendrons transported to border his own driveway, Elligott regretted and went on.

Not a soul on the road. Not a car. Not a fisherman. Not a mass-bound Catholic.

He swung into the business-center block and parked at The Pharmacy next to the grocer. The business had been sold recently by the heirs, four brothers, each more famous than the next for surliness or, as their employees explained it, they were shy. No one had ever been said good morning to by an heir. Downcast or elevated men, each on his way to transact troubling business; taking inventory; looking for dropped quarters; spider webs. They had sold out to a chain whose owners in—some said Worcester, some said Quincy—could distance themselves from light-bulb specials, jewelry deals, ad tabloids, senior-citizen discounts and generic-drug propoganda. The first act of the new owners after the opening Days of Bargains was to add a dime to the price of the Sunday *Times*.

As a businessman Elligott conceded that combination was the order of the day and somebody had to make up the premium paid for the Going Concern but not necessarily Paul D. Elligott. He would have taken his trade elsewhere, except that The Pharmacy still employed at its cash counter a pleasant man named Len who had overheard his name and very nearly remembered it. It was worth a dime to have Len say, "It's Mr Elligott. Good morning, Mr Elligott."

"How are you today, Len?"

"Gonna make it. Will that be it? One seventy-five out of two bills. Have a nice day, Mr Elligott."

Twice he had spelled it to get it right for the *Times* reservation list, but Len's memory scan rejected such an improbable reading. Elligott forgave him. Had he thought about it at the time Elligott would have written *Len* in the space on the Board of Trade questionnaire that asked for reasons he liked to shop in town: Good selections. Good prices. Good parking. Convenience. Other . . . *Len*.

Nevertheless, Elligott's acknowledging smile was of measured width. He recognized in himself a tendency to overcordiality. One of the images of Zuerner that dripped in him like a malfunctioning gland was the recollection of the day Zuerner had come aboard and been introduced around by McGlynn. Elligott had gone out to him, welcomed him warmly, braced his arm and gotten back—what would you call it: reserve? civility? The face made interesting by the scarred cheek had barely ticked.

"I look forward to working with you, Elligott."

He might have been talking to a bookkeeper instead of the Vice President Corporate Relations.

Zuerner's disfigurement conveyed the idea that something extraordinary had formed him in this way and implied that the distinction was not only external.

Since that meeting Elligott had become increasingly aware of a recompensing phenomenon that in time brought forward men who had certain kinds of injury, handicap, unhandsomeness, names; asymmetries that when they were young had put them down. Elligott had occasionally pointed out to people whom he suspected of thinking he lacked independent weight that being the namesake of the founder, even in a collateral line, might get you in at first but in the long run it was a hardship. It was difficult to be taken seriously for yourself compared to a man like Zuerner with a mark on his cheek and a bearing rehearsed to imply that he knew how to make up his mind.

In most matters whatever decision was taken, even decisions to do nothing, worked out all right if firmly asserted. Zuerner's function was to make one decision seem better than another and identify himself in this circular way as the cause of what he was in truth an effect. McGlynn had been taken in, but not Elligott.

He thought himself wiser than Zuerner by having understood him and the power cards he played. Holding back to conceal his limits. Exercises to keep from speaking early in meetings. Never answering a question if it could be reversed back on the asker.

"You've given it thought. What is your feeling?"

"Come on, Walter," Elligott had once said, "stop the crap. Just answer. I'm not asking you to invest in it."

He had been certain Zuerner would fall back from such a frank challenge. But Zuerner had maintained a steady silence that made Elligott seem petulant even to himself. Involuntarily, his face repeated its recollection of Zuerner's at their first meeting; the moment watched by McGlynn when Zuerner gained ascendancy.

At other times, when he reflected with the candor he was pleased to note in himself, Elligott conceded that the ascendancy also derived from a magical emanation from the man. There had been at Colgate an upper classman he had never exchanged a word with who had the same mysterious ascendancy. For no particular reason this Clybairne occasionally appeared in Elligott's thoughts, and Elligott felt himself stand down as he did to Zuerner.

In consideration of his move to the Cape, where he could live the personality he chose, he resolved to contain himself so that nobody would again observe his limits in the sincerity of his smile and have ascendancy over him.

Pleased by the exchange with Len and his metered response, and enjoying additionally that he had risen a notch toward the status of old-timer now that the heirs were gone, Elligott carried his newspaper next door to Dowling's.

As usual, others were there before him. He never managed to be the coffee shop's first customer. Even when he arrived at the opening minute and the door was unlocked for him there were already locals having coffee: insiders, friends of Dowling who came through the kitchen door or grew in the chairs; fungus.

Two of these insiders were at a table. He recognized them and assumed they recognized him, although they were not acquaintances, not even the order of acquaintance he would have crossed a room in a distant city to greet as compatriots; at most he might in, say, Milan have widened his eyes more generously and nodded less curtly. They returned his signal in a way that indicated they might not know him even in Nairobi.

Nobody sat at the counter, but what he thought of as his regular place at the kitchen end was cluttered by a half-finished cup of milky coffee and a cigarette burning in an ashtray. They would belong to a waitress. He disliked having to choose a stool in unfamiliar territory. He felt exposed, diminished in well-being, but was a little reassured to see that the doughnut tray had arrived from the bakery and he would not have to eat one of Dowling's double-sweet bran muffins. Brewed coffee peed into the Silex, an event that would occur in his own system given a similar excess. On the stool he arranged the *Times* in the order he would get to it: Sports, Business, Front News, The Rest.

Small impacts of alienation continued to assail him. He was not entirely used to having breakfast in a coffee shop. Men of his rank had breakfast at home. Unless they were traveling they never entered restaurants, let alone coffee shops, before lunch. Perhaps for an important early meeting but not for a doughnut. It seemed illicit, a step over the threshold to hell, a date with Sistie Evans. It took some getting used to that among the carpenters, telephone repairers, real-estate agents, and insurance men were authentic businessmen, even though retired like himself. They too had discovered late in life the pleasure of coffee and a bakery doughnut that was neither staling nor slippery; not one of those mouse-skinned packaged doughnuts.

Where was the waitress?

With the Gabberts last night the subject of best-remembered meals had come up, which led to choosing what would be ordered if you were on Death Row. When it got to him he said coffee and fresh cinnamon doughnuts.

They wouldn't accept a frivolous answer. He withdrew it. He asked Daisy to refresh him on what had been served that night at the governor's, still believing in the doughnuts and knowing in his soul that he mentioned dinner at the governor's only to tell the Gabberts there had been such an occasion. Daisy did not remember the frogs' legs as all that remarkable.

How about it Dowling? Send out the girls.

A profile appeared telepathically in the window of the kitchen door like a character on TV. A new blonde pushed in, not the dark girl with a dancer's tendony legs Elligott expected.

While she hesitated, considering whether her first duty was to her coffee and burning cigarette or to the customer, he read her marked-down face and slightly funhouse-mirror figure, the fullnesses to be made marvelously compact all her life by tights, belts, bras, girdles, panty hose and the shiny sanctifying nurse uniform Dowling provided for his staff. She would smell like an hour in a motel.

"Coffee?"

"Black. Is there a cinnamon doughnut in that tray?"

She assembled the order, remembering almost late what Dowling had told her about picking up pastry with a waxed square. Filled the cup two-thirds full. Placed the spoon with the bowl toward him. *Linda* on the tag in Mrs Dowling's childish cursives. She reached for two cream cups anyhow and showed a tunnel between her breasts. Sexuality is whatever implies more. Elligott drifted forward to fall within her odor but couldn't find it. Without drawing back from the counter she tilted her head to him intimately; it may have been something she picked up from her mother.

"Will that be all?"

Their eyes met precisely. She was no longer furniture of the establishment, she had come forward and was isolated with him.

"For now."

She closed her order book, stuffed it in the apron pocket and walked away, around the end of the counter to take up again her cigarette and milky coffee. He felt that he had opened a conversation and been rejected. When they picked up again he would not be so subtle. He could ask her where she came from, what she did before, what schedule she worked.

He scanned the newspaper through a haze of the girl, with an inattention that would have enraged the editor. Nothing about why Penn State hadn't scored with all that first-half possession he had caught a mention of on the ten o'clock news, only junk that came in before the paper went to bed: reporter's vamp on the weather and the ratatat of ball movement for the first four minutes. Nothing on Colgate but the losing score. Unimportant golf and tennis this week. Horses.

He didn't know anybody who paid attention to horses except the Derby to Belmont sequence in the spring, and the steeplechase on account of Rolling Rock and Dick Mellon. Hockey was Catholic, a real Massachusetts sport for you. Basketball was black. Nobody he knew followed those sports until the playoffs. From yesterday's paper he already knew what his stocks had done. He scanned the section all the way back to the engineer jobs and didn't see anything about Interways making a new offer for Elligott Barge. He could see her in the back-counter mirror poking at the falling-apart bundle of her hair.

He shifted the paper and looked around column one into the tunnel of her armpit. The girl was seamed with tunnels. Her raised arms drew her back erect to the position she would go down in. Women could clitter off while looking you in the eye talking about flowers, money, baked potatoes. Combing their hair, anything, just squeezing; the hidden agenda of mothers who told their little girls to keep their legs crossed. He willed the girl onto his wavelength: right guard not that many years ago at Colgate. A girl with a figure like hers wouldn't mind a little mature fattening. He watched for a sign, an eye flicker, that she was heating with him, but she finished with her hair and slumped into her mass. She seemed to have no spine. She subsided into wasted time, dribbling smoke.

He folded with a motion that caught her eye. He raised a hand to bring her to him to fill his cup, to try again to fall within her odor of cheap powder or sweat, it made no difference, and tell her that all he wanted was an hour of the thousands she had to give carelessly away. Why should he have to look for a new way to say God's first truth? In the Beginning was no more or less than this moment. It wasn't as though he had nothing to bring to the transaction, he would give more than he asked—more want, more skill, more risk. Elligott, husband, father, grandfather, retired Vice President Corporate Relations, elder, member of duty boards. More risk.

He thought of her going back to the kitchen and asking Dowling what kind of creeps he had for customers. Linda and Dowling talking about him and laughing while they challenged each other in the narrow aisle in front of the worktable. He couldn't find her odor. He imagined it from Sistie Evans forty-one years ago.

"I'll take a check."

She put it in front of him and wished him a nice day. He nodded briefly as Zuerner would have. He put the paper together again, left her a quarter more than the usual change from the dollar so she would remember him. Who was he? What did he do?

Walking out he saw that the plumber Pauley had joined the two at the table. It reminded him to go home again by Way To The Dump. The girl ceased to exist for him.

Car key poised at the lock he had a sudden disorientation. *How did I get here? Where am I going? Am I stopping or about to start? Everything is too quiet for the amount of light.* As if it were an hour ago, people weren't coming and going to get the day moving. The purity of the air and the stillness were like the moment before a tornado and everybody had taken shelter. But of course, it was Sunday, the hours were displaced. He started up and drove out of the lot.

Having grown up in the city where nature was the lawn, the hedge and the golf course, he had been slow to become available to more than the grosser performances of nature, the turning seasons and rotation of flowers. Now he saw the texture of light, predicted weather from sunsets and fuzzy moons; identified the velvet red at roadside as poison ivy, and leaves speckled like worm-infested apples as shrub cherries. He supposed that if he had gone into the landscape-gardening business he would have done well at it; better than Zuerner.

Like two daring girls back just in time from an all-night party, an apricot maple and one more golden stood in the conservative green row that shaded Pilgrim School. He rolled the window down far enough to get a better look, and then at the Betty Prior roses, the ones with a pale splash, piled along the fences. A great rose, out early and still holding; next spring he would put in a couple.

At Pauley's he slowed as he had when coming to town. So slow he might as well stop a moment and really look at the rhododendrons. He eased off the blacktop onto the shoulder. It would take only a minute to go over for a closer look. He dropped the keys on the floor as was his habit, and crossed the road.

Every finger of leaf had the thick look of health, none browned or curled in distress. Buds packed so tight it seemed they must explode before wintering. But they would hold until spring when great holiday bursts would show on the big broad-leaf plants, and the crisp varieties with small clustered leaves would light up like Christmas trees. No real rain had fallen since early July – where did they get their well-being? It wasn't likely that Pauley watered stock this fat.

Elligott bent to the ground and scratched with a forefinger. Sandy black stuff, hard and dry as his own dirt. Did the old bog leach up here to wet the roots? Elligott didn't have a bog but he had a hose and the town water bill didn't amount to much. He looked for the angle of the sun and saw that it got in here a few hours every day over the oaks beyond where the wagon was stopped. His sun at the Association got in that much.

He noticed young plants a foot or two high scattered through the hedge. Probably grown from cuttings to replace the older stock in time. Maybe layered off the big stock. He felt for a branch that might loop into the ground and come up as a new plant. No connections, must be cuttings.

Bent and reaching, Elligott now had an idea whose enormity tightened his chest. He pivoted to look both ways along the road. Carefully he opened the hedge to see the house. Shades down.

Pauley owed him something for the time he had wasted waiting for him about the shower. He grasped a plant by the throat and felt it break free of the top crust so easily that he reached for another and slung it under his arm. He looked again both ways on the road and quickly crossed.

Unlatching the tailgate delicately not to send a click into the air he laid the plants on the carpet. He was going around to the driver's door at the accelerated pace of someone not wanting to look pushy but nevertheless determined to get to the head of the line when he sensed an action at the house—a door or window opening—and somebody hollered, "What the hell are you doing there?"

Pauley's son.

He flung into the seat while the voice volleyed at him. He dragged the door closed, found the key ring on the floor, stabbed at the ignition. The lock rejected the upside-down key. He fumbled it home, jerk-started and stalled, and rammed his foot on the pedal to clear the flooded carburetor, thinking *calm! calm! breathe!* terrified that he had done himself in. He fought the key, and the engine caught at the moment frost sprang on the window lip, and he was struck on the side of the neck by what he experienced as hard-thrown gravel. He ducked and fell away from the blow and straightened again to control the careening wagon. *Get away from here fast!*

In seconds he was over a low rise and curve that blocked Pauley's place away. He realized he was locked at mach 2, rigid arms and legs shoving him hard against the seat back. He relaxed a turn and took in air. As the tension eased from his shoulder and back he became aware that his neck ached.

He put his hand to it and it came away wet. Blood thin as water defined the creases and whorls of his palm. He was not prepared for blood. So much.

He wiped his hand on his new sweater and felt the wound with his fingertips. It felt like no more than an open boil but the amount of blood scared him. He rolled his head to feel if the injury went deep. It seemed to stop at the surface. A spread of light shot? Had the man been lunatic enough to shoot because someone was poking in his bushes? What if it had been some poor bastard with bad kidneys?

Christ, look at the blood! He eased the speed and held the wheel with his bloody hand while he reached around with the other for a handkerchief, but he hadn't put one in his pocket that morning. With his knees he held the wagon enough in line, though falling toward the berm, unbuttoned his sweater, and ripped open his shirt to get cloth to plaster against the wound. He hunched his neck to cramp the cloth tight. His set changed from *Get away!* to *Where to!* and he couldn't deal with the options.

Home was four minutes away, the hospital Emergency Branch twelve by the shortcut back past Pauley's, but he couldn't even think of going back that way. The other road around the rotary was long, very long, and he was so bloody, his neck cramped awkwardly against his shoulder. He tried to remember the name of the doctor who had a shingle after the next right, and what kind of doctor he was—or should he try for a paramedic on rescue-squad duty at the firehouse left? He would have to do so much explaining. Had the wagon been identified? Just an old Chevy wagon. Who would believe it was his! His head felt enlarged, packed with engine noise and a mossy texture that resisted intelligence. It was only partly from the blow: his mind blurred in a crisis; he was not at his best at such times, he knew it, and there had never been quite such a time as this.

The corner came at him faster than he was ready. The wagon waited for direction until the last instant before lunging oversteered toward the doctor, the Association, and home almost out of habit—he never turned left there—both hands grabbing for control of the slippery wheel. The wagon bolted across the eroded center line, tires washboarding, skidding, spraying berm. His neck jarred loose from the bandage. He got back in lane while blood poured down the shoulder and sleeve of his sweater as if pumped—

As if pumped! It was more than he could get his mind around. He had just got up and gone for a cup of coffee and a doughnut and his blood was slopping out down his arm into his lap. He stuffed the wad of makeshift bandage back in

place and pressed hard against the wound; what you were
supposed to do to an artery wound—press hard. Not too long
or you would black out. An *artery*? He refused the word,
absorbed it into the moss of his head.

Dr. Albert F. Bernhardt's sign came out of the brush like a
cue card to tell him that Daisy, joking, had said a psychiatrist
lived there if they ever needed one. He raced past the psychiatrist who wouldn't know anything about blood, about *arter-
ies*, not as much as an Eagle Scout, a place to be dragged from
to somewhere else with a wagon full of blood and stolen
plants and Zuerner on the way. A curtain of weakness fell.
He wanted to let his eyes close. He sobbed to suppress the
perception that he could be dying and didn't know what to
do about Zuerner coming just in time to find out that he stole
plants in the neighborhood.

A small gray car, the first traffic on the road that morning,
closed toward him, and he roused to the thought of something better than sleep: obliteration. A smashup jumbling
and concealing everything, everything wiped out, blood
explained in bashed rolling metal and fire.

The small car came on as innocent of danger and terror as
he had himself been so short a while ago. Catholics going to
church. It would be easy; fast; over.

At the moment, the only moment he had, he was incapable
of aiming. He felt a blurt of nobility as the car went by. Did
they see the blood? Did they think he held his head this way
because he was sleepy? Did they know he held their lives in
his hand for a moment and was merciful? He was a merciful
man with no possession in the world but mercy—and to
strangers—and nobody was there to sign his card.

The wagon was at the fork where the Association road
came in. Barely driven, it was taking him home to tell Daisy
to cover him from Zuerner. Daisy would clean up everything
and make it plausible. He found the least strength necessary
to guide onto the sudden rough and sounding surface.

He couldn't bother to steer around potholes. He went
down the crown of the dirt road, jouncing and pounding the

shocks, slack hand on the wheel like a dozing passenger. At the turn-off to his own driveway he knew he wasn't going to get to Daisy. He was gone, he didn't have have time to tell Daisy what she had to do. He was going to pass out. In a gravel-scattering skid he entered his own long curving drive at forty, forty-five, fifty toward the open garage door that waited to swallow him against the far wall and create a mystery—heart attack? pedal stuck?—his name intact.

Elligott now had his last great idea of the morning.

Alongside the garage the land sloped to the cove through an insubstantial hedge of nursery plants—forsythia, hydrangea, cinquefoil and the like—and lower down, wild honeysuckle, briar and saplings that had volunteered to try again where the city people had cleared. At the foot the returning tide infiltrated the bordering marsh grass.

The possibility came to him almost too late to act on. With nothing measurable to spare he veered past the corner of the garage, over the sunk railroad tie that defined the hedge line, trashed the nursery row, trashed the honeysuckle, flailed through a berserk car wash of saplings, briar, rugosas, grapevines, forcing all the momentum he could into the wagon to scar through the soft wetland and into the cove where the thrust ended abruptly, yet gently, like a boat with a sail dropped.

The wagon tilted on a rock and stopped.

He would have to stay in motion to keep from blacking out. He pulled the latch; his weight pushed the door open and he slumped with it clumsily into a tide that took him at the knee. By noon it would be chest-high. He steadied on the door. Everything was quiet after the last tearing minutes. *Forget the plants. Can't lift the door. Not unusual to carry plants in the wagon. Water will make a slop back there, mix everything up. Keep moving.*

He staggered around the drowning wagon, slipping on bottom rocks greasy with eelgrass. He glanced up at his house. Through sagging eyelids he saw that it was handsome in the early sun. He started to take his hand from the bloody bundle at his neck so he could look at his watch and verify the time but knew at once it was an act too foolish to complete. If only Daisy would appear and they could wave goodbye to each other—

Crouched, balancing with his free arm like the remembered sepia picture of a farmer scattering grain, he lurched against the heavy purpose of the tide, toward no vision of a farther life or of beings natural or supernatural intended to be called up by ten thousand Sunday-morning mumblings. That and all love, error and regret; all papers on his desk, all letters, all unkempt plantings, all things unsaid to Daisy and Margie and the grandchildren and the judge in the traffic court: gone, irretrievable. His last mercy dispensed. His last desire a girl in a doughnut shop. His last act theft. Only honor now was left to him.

His new sweater sucked up a weight of water. He swayed and stumbled over the unstable bottom. His eyes closed to a minimum blur of light and form. His head hung forward. The hand that held the blood-wet cloth failed to his side. He dragged one more step, and another, and another toward the obscure channel hidden in the grass over there where an hour ago he had foreseen sneaking the net under big blue crabs so Zuerner would sign his card. Elligott, a man whose name had decided his work and chosen his wife; and she had brought him to this place where a stranger with a gun decided when he was to die.

Or was it Zuerner, who would follow him everywhere, who had decided? Caving to his knees, fainting, falling toward drowning, his impression (the vapor of exhaustion could no longer be called something as coherent as thought)—his impression was that to die this worthily was an act of transcendant honor; beyond the comprehension of a man like Zuerner. And yet, the vapor formed, faded: what is Zuerner to me that I give him my life?

Clay Carter's Will

1

"I'LL help you hang the show."

"You were going to work on your boat."

"I'll do the show. I can get to the boat next week. Give me my marching orders."

Vi could get somebody else but with him she could change her mind, she could be cranky; marriage allowed for that. Marriage was an agreement to stick together come hell or high water, and get on with the main jobs: sex, cooking, children, talking safely about other people, being reasonable about money. And in order to get on with it, to put up with each other's humanity—crankiness, mind-changing, leaving the famous toilet seat up, under-cooking hard-boiled eggs; transgressions that from anyone else would annoy the hell out of you.

The agreement could have been made with somebody else (unless it were really true that marriages were made in heaven, which would be like dying and finding out that Dante and Billy Sunday had it about right) but it was made between those two, and these were the only two people in the world who had an unlimited call on each other:

—including forgiveness, because everybody required continual forgiveness—for everything from being late to putting the newspaper together out of order—and only saints had enough forgiveness for the whole race. Everything began with these two.

Clay had explained all that to her because everybody didn't think things through as he did. Everybody had an instinct for what marriage was, but they didn't define it, "and if they don't define it" (he said *they* when he meant *you*, but *you* was confrontational, and marriage was intended to avoid confrontation) "then they don't understand what they're into, and those marriages don't survive the crunches."

"That's how it is," Vi said.

"Millions of women can cook. Millions of men can make a living. You were romanced by terrific men. I had fantastic women. So why are we two married?"

"You asked me."

"You could have said no."

"I loved you. You've told me many times you loved me. We love each other, don't we?"

"For me, after thirty years, more than ever. I understand now that love is even more than I used to think it was."

He didn't tell her what love is and was and she didn't ask because that too was part of their agreement: that he would walk an idea twice around the block if he didn't stop himself, and beyond a certain line she dealt in image and instinct.

Vi said, "In the morning the Acceptance Committee is taking in the pictures. I get the room from one o'clock. I told them I was going to lock the door and wouldn't take anything in. I had enough of that mañana gang."

They drove up to Williston's narrowset clapboard barn, now the Mid-Cape Art Center courtesy of a grant from the state obtained through the persistence of Ina Prell. Ina's husband was president of the League for Economy in Government. He would have routinely sent a letter to his legislator, copy to the editor, opposing the grant as another waste of taxpayer's money, except that it was Ina's project, and like Clay Carter he knew that in marriage you closed your eyes to some things.

The chairman of the Acceptance Committee passed on the baton. "We have eighty-four pieces from fifty-two exhibitors. Every one is wired for hanging except Eunice Madden's."

"Of course," Vi said, referring to Eunice.

"She didn't have any screw eyes. She said she didn't care if you just leaned it against the wall."

"Of course," Vi said. She closed the door behind the Acceptance Committee and looked at her watch. He already had looked at his.

"One o'clock on the button," Clay said. "Do you want me to wire this one or do you want to lean it against the wall?"

"Put it in the closet over there. Everybody knew this show was to be hung, not leaned, and we are not doing any wiring. We are hanging." She wasn't married to Eunice Madden.

The skylighted space was a pleasant environment. On the wide-plank walls she would have preferred a lesser white — something with an earthtone — but it would work out all right; the show was oils, no glass would gather stark reflections. Waiting on her judgment of how they should be sequenced and hung, paintings were stacked along the walls and the display panels that quartered the room.

She began to walk slowly, looking at the art with exact vision. Watching for a few moments her compact well-formed figure disciplined in a closely-fitted skirt, her face summer-darkened toward the umber of her simply cut hair, Clay knew he had chosen well: a wife, the mother of his children, a woman others trusted to act responsibly without regard to friendship or politics.

She shifted two pieces to make an opening and brought one from farther along to fill the vacancy. "It's going to take me a while."

"When you're ready."

He pulled a chair up to the table that tomorrow would have the price sheets, punch bowl, wine, grapes, goldfish crackers, chutney-covered cream cheese, peanuts (mixed nuts on high holidays) ginger snaps, and — if the hospitality chairman was a good one — a snack as new and memorable as the chutney-covered cream cheese once had been. He played a client's tax problem on his pocket calculator. He made notes on the pad in the cover. The time would not be wasted. He was an efficient man, made like Fred Astaire with nothing to spare. Enough pale hair had been provided to cover his head, enough muscle and skin to cover his bones. His belt size had changed once since their marriage; he had resolved it would not change again. Both his parents died in their sixties and he could not rely on genes alone to get him more than the biblical allotment.

He lived right—as he finished the calculation she said, "Okay, let's get 'em up."

His assignment was to locate the hanging point on the wall and hoist the picture into place so she could see if she was comfortable with the weightiness, size, color, subject and framing of each picture compared to those adjoining. What looked at first as if it would work, sometimes didn't; hanging a show was like trying on hats or shoes.

At the place she chose to begin Clay held a picture to the wall, a rather nice sunset on the bay, he thought. He was often amazed that in the middle of Cape Cod—not Provincetown—were so many painters who seemed to know how to get what they were after. A few sold a few dollars' worth, a few sold a few hundred or like Vi a few thousand dollars' worth.

Those like Gilbert Asmer who sold many thousands of dollars' worth did not have their work in these shows. It was their livelihood. Gil had his own gallery. But looking at Gil's work and, say, Thelma Snyder's, who painted the same kind of fuzzed-up scene with smashes of color here and there and sold a picture now and then, you had to think that who was chosen and who was not was significantly accidental.

At art occasions Clay often reflected that this was why there was life on earth, to express yourself in pictures or music or poems, to govern, to teach, to know the names of plants in a garden, to succor the wounded, to do more than make enough money to get comfortably to the grave. He wished he could do something like that better than he did. He wished he had stayed with the clarinet. Well, at least he understood these things. Understanding was not only a pleasure, it was a function; they needed him too.

She said, "Right there."

He kept the end of his middle finger on the wall where the

brad of the hanger should be driven. If the ceiling had not been so high, he would have faced the picture to the wall and measured down to the wire with a stiff tape.

With his free hand he propped the painting against his leg, took a hanger from his breast pocket, gave it to the hand against the wall, took the hammer out of his belt, drove the brad not quite home; if he was wrong, a claw could get hold of it.

He raised the picture, caught the end of the wire in the hanger and slid it to approximate center. As he was too close to judge, she coached from a distance to get it square. After he finished hammering his way around the room they would all be jarred cockeyed again, but she liked to see them square right away. All right, whatever she liked.

The first picture was easy. From then on it could be a dog-fight. They had eighty-four—now eighty-three—pictures to hang. Vi had no sense of time. She didn't realize that even if they went along at express rate it would take three hours, she would be dead tired. It was up to him to save enough min-utes to pick up a half-hour.

She said, "I think we ought to get this one lined up at the top with the other."

He warned her, "It will bother your eye if I'm a quarter-inch off." She should try anything but lining them up. It would be pure luck if he got it right the first time. It would slow them down.

"Just this once. They'll make a good block together. A little left. More. That's it."

He set, drove, and hung. Right the first time, a good omen. "Next."

They worked their way around the gallery, sustained by diet colas and a package of trail food. They talked about their children who lived in distant cities. They talked about the Henrys, who were getting a divorce, and about Phil Freeder, who was marrying again, good for him. They talked about art, which is how he had come to know expressionism from hamburger, and about artists, with many of whom he now had acquaintance. He was even able to recognize a few by their work without having to find their signatures.

They came to her entry, a scene in her peculiarly angular manner, the house narrower and taller than reality and the colors laid down in strong vertical panels. A signature was seldom needed to identify Vivian Carter's paintings. He liked the painting as he liked most of her work.

"You picked a good one."

"Not for this judge. Selma Kay likes soft edges."

"You still picked a good one."

They were two hours into it and he saw she was beginning to flag. Her cheeks sagged. Her conversation was getting short. Saving energy, she wouldn't talk about anything but up, down or a little left.

"Why don't you take a break and wash your face? You'll feel better."

"I want to finish."

"You'll feel better."

"Move it a touch left."

He moved, drove the hanger, leveled and was about to move to the next space when the painting he had just hung caught his eye. It seemed a familiar landscape. He had not been paying much attention to the art as he was too close to see it well, and he would have time later and at the opening tomorrow. But this painting caught him.

The scene was from their bedroom window. It had not been painted by Vi. He read the bold signature of Nelson Phinley, a name he thought he had heard but could not place. No mistaking the corner of the window frame itself, the oak limb crossing, and beyond, the cedars standing at the great round rock it had taken a glacier to move into the salt marsh, all included with nearly photographic precision.

He had stood at that window many times, throwing a knot into his tie or raising the blind to look at the morning weather. He had stood there with his arm on Vi's shoulder, watching the sunset paint the marsh.

Puzzled, censoring the impulse to make a comment of recognition that he would have made if the signature had been a
woman's, he went on with the rest of his assignment while he
mulled the oddity that a man he didn't know had painted a
scene looking out his bedroom window.

When they finished hanging they walked the room again to
level the paintings and place identifying numbers. He
maneuvered not to be at the wall with the Phinley painting
while Vi worked there, and he showed no deliberate attention to it when he had an opportunity to walk by again and
verify the name: Nelson Phinley.

She stood at the door to take it all in as somebody entering
for the first time, saw it was well hung, and quit. Too tired
even to photograph a record of her work, she sat at the
cream-cheese and chutney table, heels eased out of her
shoes, finishing her Coke while his camera blinked around
the room wall by wall, panel by panel, till the roll was shot
off. They went home, and from the bedroom window he
verified the scene.

The following day at the opening he looked for Phinley,
and soon found him, a rather short younger man standing in
front of his painting, receiving greetings and compliments
from his friends. He had the engaging manner of a man who
had stories to tell and knew others wanted to hear them.

Vi moved from one cell of artists to another, speaking of
their work and coming shows. If he knew the group, Clay
entered it, otherwise he found other husbands or, as he was
well-known and had a prominent practice in accountancy,
they found him. The judge had come in that morning and
done her work. Carter studied the ribboned winners, trying
to understand why these and not others, and did not entirely
succeed. He tried the wine and the nutted cheeseball and a
cracker. He skipped the pretzels, potato chips, punch and
cookies.

Phinley did not come his way, and Clay did not seek him
out. Vi and Phinley were in a group at one time. She gave
him no particular attention, laughed once at something he

said, but only as the others did, and soon moved to another group.

In an hour she caught her husband's eye and raised her eyebrows, which in some contexts meant what do you think? and in this meant she had had enough, shall we go?

In the succeeding weeks and months—which became years—Clay Carter was many times in the company of the man who had painted a scene from his bedroom window. They said a word or two. They nodded to each other at the post office. Phinley was a bachelor, an expert draftsman, which explained the precision of his painting. He had come to town from Hartford, recruited by an architect who assured him that the profession was flat-out on the Cape and he would find a lot of work, which was true.

Vi mentioned Phinley's name when there was an occasion (he was on a committee, he had a show at the Conservatory, he was giving a course in landscape) but only as she mentioned others; not seeking to say his name, as was the habit of lovers, nor avoiding it, so that if Clay had not known otherwise, Phinley would have had no extraordinary presence.

Yet he knew otherwise. She had betrayed him, but with such consideration for his feelings that he could not bring himself to challenge her. No less than before, in bed, or in the company of their children or friends, or in companionable trips to Paris and Madrid or to the galleries in Boston and New York, or in the ordinary course of living together—never did she in the least support a suspicion that another man had been in her bedroom.

And if she so well dissembled that occasion, was it still going on? Were there others?

He considered how much that was good would be destroyed if he required her to face him on it, and decided no, it was in their compact that he would forgive.

But it was difficult to forgive what was not confessed, for it remained unfinished, and it was not fitting that he be the one to bring it up. That was hers to do. He was not a policeman. It was not discovery but confession freely offered that would make them whole again. He tried to see it as she must—an addition to her life, not a diminution of their marriage which went on as before.

Many times his impulse to instruct her in the nuance of the matter, which he saw with such clarity, brought him to the verge of saying, "The marriage compact provides a way even for infidelity to be accommodated, but probably not if it is a continuing phenomenon. An interjection can be thought of as no more than a vacation. However, a parallel structure—" He had difficulty formulating it.

The failed conversation opened his mind to possibilities he would otherwise not have considered.

At the party celebrating the election of the right people to the Board of Selectmen, Clay saw, over the shoulder of a member of the town Finance Committee, Phinley come away from the buffet table with a drink and a plate of hors d'ouevres and take a seat on a hassock alongside Vi's chair. She tucked her skirt tight to make room. They fiddled with the drinks and the food while they held a quiet head-down discussion without looking at each other.

Clay was touched by anger at his exclusion. They must mistake his forbearance for stupidity. Undoubtedly there were people in the room who knew more than they should about Vi Carter and Nelson Phinley. Vi was not so considerate of his feelings as he had at first thought. Infidelity with a cowboy in Arizona or the curator of an upstate museum was something that could be distanced, but Nelson Phinley walking around South Westham with guilty knowledge was an invasion of his privacy. Not for any reason at all should Vi have positioned her husband to be thought stupid by an outsider to their marriage. He went to the buffet and folded a tissue of roast beef on a chip of rye bread. Maureen Dahl Slater moved in alongside.

"Clay, we never talk. You're such an interesting man and we never talk."

"Talk," he said. He selected the creamier of two mustards.

"If you put the mustard on top it gets on your lips."

"Good thinking." They had had two drinks. She harvested celery, carrot strips, corn relish, mushrooms and a new brand of toast that was too large to eat entire and would shatter if bitten.

"I never saw these before," she said, holding a toast for his examination. "Listen, Clay, do you do income tax for plain people like me?"

"Who thinks Maureen Dahl Slater is plain people?"

Really she was plain, but flamboyantly. Her fiftyish figure was slightly excessive. Her eyes were set in dark patches as if she had walked into a door last night. She wore several strands of chewy-looking pearls; small saltwater taffies. The bronzy silky dress fell in tiers. When the Cape Jazz Company put on its show at the Yacht Club, that was Maureen Dahl Slater on drums, and good. Still, she seemed a simple, straight-up kind of person who didn't push for attention. She had good calves. She did summer rentals for Central Cape Realty.

"I've got a letter from the IRS. I don't know what they want. Somebody has to take charge of me. Would you do that?"

"That's what I get paid for. Give me a call."

"Like tomorrow?"

Tomorrow he didn't have two drinks. He decided that he felt like a man who had been off cigarettes for a year and had too big an investment in abstinence to light up for a casual reason. He did her taxes.

2

Clay and Vi Carter were getting on toward elderly when, reviewing his will, a way occurred to him to settle the matter on terms that avoided confrontation but still must give her significant pause, and if they should meet in another life (if there were another life of an agreeable kind) that would enable them to smile conjugally at the anecdote.

The idea did not stale with time or fulfill itself in the conception as cleverness often did. Getting there was only half the fun—the rest remained to do.

He watched the obituaries in the Boston paper until one day the untimely death of Annalee Claire Summers was reported, a teacher in Newton schools, ten years younger than himself, much loved by students and associates. Annalee had never married. The photograph showed her to be a good-looking woman, capable of vivacity. Eight years ago Miss Summers had been runner-up in Newton senior women's tennis. She was survived by married and single sisters, and parents.

A picture formed in his mind of a handsome well-adjusted athletic intelligent woman from a large and loving family who for one reason or another happened not to marry. In a way, what he had in mind to do would say something appropriate in the circumstances not only about his life but about hers. A romantic legend would be created in her family. The novelty of the idea enthused him.

Telling Vi he had to be in Boston on client business, he drove to Newton, inquired at the pharmacy for directions to the 300 block of North Walcott, and soon was in the lesser but substantial neighborhood of the affluent town, cruising a street much as he had imagined. The plain front-porched houses had been built sixty or seventy years ago for families that put away money steadily. Children had lived at home, sometimes when married, often into long spinsterhoods and bachelorhoods.

The shingled turret marked the slate-gray house at 360 as somewhat older, one of the deans of the street. The small lawn had long ago been overruled by the shade and arching roots of a maple, now too fine to be taken down no matter how ill-advised the first owner had been to encourage its sapling years. On the porch was a stroller, signifying that the good years of number 360 were not all used up.

He went to the town center and had a sandwich and came back for another look before heading home. The stroller was gone but farther down the street it came toward him wheeled by a woman too old to be the mother of a toddler unless she had been greatly surprised. A grandmother or an aunt. When she glanced up as he passed he had the impression of a woman who held a good job taking her day off—a teacher, a competent clerk of a court. She had good features and carried herself with strength. That became for him the look of Annalee.

Clay went in to see Joe Lynch who lived and practised in Hyannis, outside the circle of Carter familiars.

"I want to add a name to those who get specific bequests. A Miss Annalee—A N N A L E E—Claire—with an E on the end—Summers—S U M M E R S of three-sixty North Walcott Street, Newton Mass."

The lawyer had it down on his yellow pad. "What is the bequest?"

"A hundred thousand dollars."

A significant amount, the lawyer thought, but he knew from transactions that had gone through his office that Carter had done well in land investments. Many men connected second- and third-hand to Cape Cod real estate had done well, and easy prosperity led some that he knew into second lives. Lynch himself had something going with a woman who owned a dress shop in Centerville and had come to him about a matter with her landlord. Lynch did not jump to a conclusion. Lawyers of all people were well aware that things were not always what they seemed. Annalee Claire Summers might be a relative who for any number of reasons was considered benevolently.

"Is there anything else I should know?"

"If Miss Summers dies before me, nothing is to go to her heirs. Everything in that case stays in my estate."

"No problem. Anything else?"

"You have to do me a favor. I want this dated back two years."

Lynch didn't like to go off the main road unless he had to. The least irregularity had the knack of snagging on something going by, leading to unforeseen complications that required repair. "What's your problem? There might be a better way."

"Do it that way, Joe, if you don't mind. I've given it a lot of thought. I would really like to do it that way."

It was done that way.

When Clay died, a son-in-law who had made an enormously lucky investment in an electronics company and thereafter had the respect due a witch doctor who happened to eat the heart of a deer on the morning the chief's fever broke, assumed the role of the financial head of the family. His brother-in-law, although older, worked in an agency that tested the degree of disablement of handicapped children.

"Do you have a copy of the will?" the witch doctor asked Vi.

She looked in the drawer where Clay kept papers. Her will was there but not Clay's. It might be in the box at the bank.

"Don't touch the box. The IRS will suspect that you took out the crown jewels or bearer bonds. If the bank is on the ball they have the box sealed and won't even let you look." He read the lawyer's name off the sleeve of the will. "Would Lynch have been Dad's lawyer?"

Lynch was the only lawyer she knew about.

The son-in-law met Lynch at the funeral and asked for a copy of the will. Vi had it in the mail the next morning. She read first in bewilderment, then with the helpless rage of a battered woman who had no recourse anywhere. Clay had left money to a woman she had never heard of. She had not suspected or even imagined a woman in his life. What was she to think but the obvious?

Past mourning, she brought the document to the lunch table and laid it first before her older daughter. "Read that," she instructed. Her daughter made a thoughtful face before handing it to her sister. The sons-in-law had the gist before it became their turn to read. They had the marginal discomfort of supposing they were by gender implicated in Vi's displeasure.

"Let me see what I can find out," the witch doctor said. "I'll talk to Lynch and see what he knows."

"He is not to think that I am in any way surprised or unhappy," Vi said balefully.

Lynch said that he knew no more than they all now knew. As the executor he would put the will before the court for probate, notify the heirs, have the bank add up the assets and obligations. Debts would be paid and in more or less a year the estate would be distributed.

He cautiously volunteered information beyond what was at the moment absolutely necessary.

"If the will is contested by anyone—say Miss Summers or—or—" he thought of another beneficiary to put it in scale—"the University of New Hampshire—or—" an afterthought "even Mrs Carter for any reason, it should be born in mind that I represent the estate and would have to defend it. The contestant would have to proceed through another lawyer."

"I understand." He did not allow it to be thought that he did not already understand whatever was said. "I'm only trying to get as much information together as I can before I go back to Denver."

"Tell your mother-in-law to pick up the phone any time she wants to talk to me."

The daughters counseled, "Don't let it get to you, Mother. You can live without the money. Remember, you and Dad had it together, better than almost anybody."

Every day the widow was getting more used to it. "I'm simmering down. I just wish there hadn't been any will. I wish I hadn't known. I'm not going to let it bother me very much."

One daughter said to the other, "I don't understand Dad getting involved in something like this or letting it come out this way. Why didn't he make a settlement on her off the books if it came to that?"

"He didn't consult me. If he had been my husband instead of my father I would have murdered him."

Contrary to Joe Lynch's natural concern there were no

snags, although the situation was different from what he had supposed. The paper addressed to Annalee Claire Summers at the Newton address came back signed by the guardian of a seven-year-old child, with a note saying he assumed that was the Annalee Claire Summers intended. Lynch thought it would be a good idea to hire an investigator to work up the Summers situation.

One Annalee Claire Summers was already dead when the codicil was written and backdated. Clay Carter would have known that. Lynch didn't have to say anything about it.

Clay must have meant the child Annalee, the niece. Born to a cousin of the deceased Annalee and an unknown man, she had been taken in by this generous and compassionate family. The identity of the unknown father might now be guessed.

The hundred thousand was the child's unless the question was raised that her aunt was the intended beneficiary, in which case it would have to be contended that the bequest should revert to the estate and nothing should go to the child. Joe Lynch did not want to be the lawyer who tried to convince a judge or jury or anybody on the street that the child was cut out of the will.

He was, however, bound to explain about the two Annalees to Vivian. He discreetly went over again the implication of a contest.

"Oh Lord, I have no reason to do any such thing," Vi said. "It was the way Clay wanted it."

Lynch mentioned that down the road a question of support might arise. He suggested that she might want to review the language of her own will in order to protect the estate intended for the children of Clay and Vivian Carter.

3

Vi had many friends with whom she continued to paint and go to galleries. She enjoyed her children and the grandchildren who came to visit her on Cape Cod and sail in the bay and swim off Great Beach.

At times she had an impulse to let it be known that she would not mind welcoming Clay's Annalee here, but overruled it as not the best of ideas. The child was not her blood. Let her children and grandchildren whose blood Annalee was deal with it. It was enough to know that the child was being raised in a good family. Who knew what can of worms an unnecessary inquiry might open. If anything occurred in the future that would bring her and Annalee together, Vi resolved to be available for it.

She remained in good health and lived in the big house for the rest of her days. Everybody was invited to drop in there after the memorial service in the Church of the Holy Spirit.

Her friends came and looked at her paintings, and those of other artists whose work she had admired and bought or exchanged for her own. They introduced themselves to her children and told them what wonderful parents Clay and Vi must have been, and how lucky they were to have had their mother so long. Some had painted with Vivian.

The children recalled a dapper easy-chatting old gaffer who told them he had come to town a stranger—

"I showed up at a meeting of the art association. Most of them were women, and I guess they wanted to have another live man on hand to do heavy lifting. They were quite open. When I asked where you paint around here, your mother reached out a handful of photographs from her carryall and gave them to me. 'Here, these will get you started,' she said. I made a living off your mother's photos until I got around enough to shoot my own. You always knew where you stood with your mother. If you asked her what she thought of your work she'd tell you. You could believe her. She was the best kind of friend."

Before the service the sons-in-law, identified as such to strangers by their boutonnieres, striped pants and oxford jackets with sleeves covering their wrists and more, had taken positions in the foyer of the church. Monitoring the Book of Remembrance the witch doctor had noted the name Annalee Claire McDaniels too late to greet her meaningfully. He was quite sure, however, that he had identified her at the end of a pew, alone. He looked for her at the reception but she was not there. He was able to tell his wife—how many Annalee Claires could there be in this world?—that the young woman had a pronounced resemblance to her father.

Dog People

SOMETIMES when Allan Stonnier drove out and the dogs were there he revved up and aimed. He could do it because he had an agreement with them that no matter how disdainfully they stood their ground they would at the last moment lurch out of range if he went no more than a certain speed. The time he brushed McCoors's brown dog he felt bad about it but the dog hadn't cooperated. He was too cocky. Stonnier had nothing against the dog. How could a man have anything against a dog? After that when he revved up he was ready to shift to the brake fast.

McCoors was coming through his woodlot and saw Stonier drive at the dogs. he said "If you ever hit one of my dogs I'll break your fucking head."

"I wouldn't hit your dogs. I just want to scare them. Keep your dogs off my property. You have land."

"I'll break your fucking head."

"I'll be where you can find me."

That was a long time ago, when you could still talk to people about their dogs.

This morning Stonnier was out early and running. A usual Cape Cod spring, more evident on calendars from the hardware store than on the land. A dry northeaster thrashed the guard of unleafed oak, cherry and locust. An incontinent snow patch, sprawled like an dirty old sheep dog on the lea side of the downed pine, drained toward the dozer-cut that had made Stonnier's lane forty years ago. Stonnier's running shoes threw wet sand from runnels. He took in all the air his chest and belly would hold; he had been a runner since making the mile-relay team at Nauset Regional, and had known all that time that even if you didn't want to breathe at all you had to fill up.

The air held the thaw of dogshit banked over the winter by neighbor dogs on his paths and driveway lane, in his mow field and kitchen garden; butts and drools and knobs of it, clumped grains and hamburgers of it indistinguishable except in shape from their previous incarnation in bags and cans. Stonnier couldn't see how a dog took any nourishment from it. It looked the same coming as going. No wonder they used so much. The companies owned two of the big networks. From time to time the deposits were withdrawn on Stonnier's rakes and shoes; were wheeled into the garage on the tires of his Ford hatchback. Verna's glove gathered it in the seagrass mulch on the asparagus. He didn't need it. He would have been better off to have set out a little later and got a sun high enough to define the footing better.

By his look he had seventy-or-so disciplined years on him; a man of medium height, bony, with a cleaving profile; a fisherman by trade before he had the stake to buy The Fish & Chips. He loped out the lane evasively like a football player training on a course of automobile tires.

When it still was possible to speak to people about their dogs Verna had said "You could talk to him. He probably doesn't realize."

How couldn't he realize? He left the dogs to run all day while he and his wife were away in their store. What did he think the dogs did with what he put in them when he turned them out in the morning?

McCoors said he didn't think they were his dogs did it. He said he would keep an eye on them. He tied them. They barked. They barked from eight o'clock when he left until six when he came home and let them run until dark. Allan skipped a stone at them a couple of times to let them know he didn't want them near his house. They stayed beyond the turn in the driveway so he wouldn't see them.

Stonnier encountered McCoors one day when they both were looking for their property bounds. He mentioned that the dogs barked all day and McCoors might not know it as he was away.

McCoors said if you tie up dogs they bark. He tied them up to please Stonnier. Now Stonnier was complaining again. McCoors broke off the conversation and walked away. McCoors had a tough body, and eyes that quickly turned mean. Allan told Verna the man reminded him of a prison guard. "I guess there are all kinds of looking prison guards but McCoors is what I think of. That's nothing against prison guards." On no later than second thought Stonnier always tried to be fair.

Deakler, another two-dog man, bought the place on the other side of the hill. His dogs came over to find out about McCoors's dogs at the same time McCoors's dogs came over to investigate the new neighbors. They met on Stonnier's driveway where it joined the Association lane, smelled each other, peed on the young azaleas Stonnier had raised from cutting in tin cans, and agreed to meet there each day when their food was sufficiently digested. Wahlerson's half-chow and Paul's black newfie heard about the club and came up the Association road to join.

Stonnier spoke to Deakler.

Deakler was an affable man who had been sales vice president of a generator reconditioning company and knew how to get along while not giving in. "Well you know how it is with dogs. You don't want to keep a dog tied up all the time. That's why we moved out here."

Stonnier said he shouldn't have to take care of other people's dog dirt.

"Shoo them off if they bother you. Do them good."

"They scare my granddaughter when she visits. They charge."

"They never bit anybody. People have dogs. She should get used to them."

"That's up to her if she wants to get used to dogs charging

and growling at her. I had dogs. I like dogs. I have nothing against your dogs. They should stay on their own property. Is that a communist idea?"

Deakler looked at him speculatively; as if it might be.

"I don't like to quarrel with neighbors," Stonnier said. "We'll have to see. There's a leash law. I don't like to be talking law."

Stonnier already knew from the Small Animal Officer that if there was a dog you couldn't keep off your property you had to catch him before you called for somebody to take him away. "You don't have to catch your own bank robbers," Stonnier said. The SAO said "That's how the town wants it, don't talk to me."

"Laws are one thing," Deakler said. "This is all Association property. Private property. You don't have to leash your dog if it's on private property." The leash law didn't even run in the Association because the whole Association was private, including the beach and the roads which all the private property owners owned in common; privately. "That's why I came out here," Deakler said. "It isn't all closed in like it is in town."

Stonnier hadn't thought about that. "What if I brought a big potty over to your house every day and dumped it in your yard?"

The two-dog man didn't think that was much of an argument. Stonnier brought it up at the Association meeting in July. Oh, that was twenty-two years ago, how time flies. He remembered getting up to speak to the others on Giusti's patio. He had not in his lifetime before—or later—often spoken in meetings of that size. He thought he could remember every time. Three times at town meeting—about the algae on the pond and the proposed parking ordinance and the newspaper not printing what the Otter River Bank was doing on mortgages—and at the Board of Trade about extending town water to the new subdivisions. Subjects that affected him. His house. His business. That's how the world worked. You spoke for yourself, and if you made sense others voted with you even if it might go a little against their own interests. That's how he always voted. He didn't sign petitions for things like the new children's park because he didn't sign petitions if he could avoid admitting that he noticed the lady with the clipboard at the post office, but he voted for it. The Taxpayer's Association said it put points on the tax bill. That's all right, it still made sense that the kids have a place with a fence around where dogs couldn't get in. It was the way he would want it for his own grandchildren if they lived in town. A few years back he would have asked, "Why don't they fence in the dogs and let the kids run?," but you couldn't ask anything like that anymore.

Mostly he jogged these days. He paced an easy 120, waiting for his body to tell him how hard he could run. It wasn't his heart, it was his back; were the tendons and nerves lined up so the jolt passed through like smoke and went off into the air or would it jam somewhere on his hip or fourth vertebrae? He told Verna, "He says it's in the vertebrae but that's not where I feel it. They knew all about hearts but they didn't know anything about backs except rest it." They told his father and his grandfather the same damn thing. He felt secure and let out to 130.

He had thought his statement that he had nothing against dogs but that the town leash law ought to run in the Association would appeal to reasonable people. The dogs tramped down the lettuce, shat so you couldn't trust where to walk after dark, chased cars, growled at strangers. He didn't say shat, he said Did their business. Somebody said "They doo-doo on your Brooks Brothers shoes," a reference to a man who at that time was running to be president of the country, and everybody laughed except Morrison and Dannels, who were large contributors to the candidate's committee. Halfway along into the laughter Stonnier caught on and joined to show his fellowship although he sensed it took the edge off the seriousness of his argument.

He had expected David Haseley would say something. Haseley had several times mentioned to him—or agreed with him—that the dogs were out of hand. As a retired high officer of a very large business in Cleveland, Haseley's views were taken into account, but he chose not to speak to the motion. Only Larry Henry's widow Marcia spoke for it. Verna had been good to Marcia, shopped for her, looked in on her when she was laid up.

Sensing the anger of their neighbors who spoke of liberties being taken from people everywhere and now this, the summer people kept quiet or voted with the dog people. The aye's lacked the assertive spine of the no's. Stonnier thought most members hadn't voted and that it might be different in a written ballot, but it didn't seem to be the way to press an issue among neighbors.

In a spirit of goodwill there was then a unanimous *Yes* on a resolution that people were responsible for their own dogs. It did not specify how the responsibility should be manifested.

After the meeting he said to Haseley he would have thought more people would be for the leash law. Haseley nodded in the meditative, prudential manner that had earned him his good name and said, "Yes that's so." It could have meant I agree with you, that's what you thought. People didn't use words like they used to. Allan's mother had instructed him to speak up and say as best he could what he meant so people knew what was on his mind. Now you had to be sure you asked the right question or you might not even get close to what they really thought. Everybody seemed to think it was all right.

Stonnier hadn't pressed Haseley. He felt diffident toward him not only on account of his bearing but because the older man was of the management class as were all the others in the Association but himself. They were vice presidents, deans, professors, proprietors, accountants, lawyers; immigrants from Providence, Amherst, Ohio, Pennsylvania; taxed, many of them, in Florida, which the Stonniers had visited in their camper but had not been taken by sufficiently to give it six months and a day every year. The others had all gone beyond high school.

"I still don't know how Haseley voted," he told Verna.

Allan and Verna Stonnier were second-generation Cape Cod, the only native-born in the West Bay Association, the first to raise children there and see them bussed to school in Orleans and then go out on their own. Allan had done well with The Fish & Chips — better than such a modest-looking enterprise implied — but he remained somewhat apart from the others. His three-acre parcel on the waterfront cost under three thousand dollars when it was a half-mile bounce in the rut to get out there. After the fire at The Fish & Chips ten years ago the real estate woman who called about buying the lot asked about the house too. She had a customer she thought would pay more than a million dollars if Allan would consider selling. They thought he would sell his house and get out but nothing could make him move after the fire. He was so set that Verna had to make it half a joke when she said that with a million dollars and the insurance from the fire they could live anywhere they wanted. By now it might be up to two million, the way prices were. He knew it as well as she did, and if he wanted to talk about it he would say so. "It's the whole country," he said. Everywhere. You might as well deal with it where you are. A million dollars after tax wasn't all that much anymore anyhow.

McCoors's two dogs came out to yap at him. He said *Yah* and raised his elbow and they shut up and backed off while he padded on toward the wider graveled lane that looped through the fifty-three properties in the West Bay Association and carried their cars to the blacktop and town.

Shoeman's black-and-white sort-of-spitz bitch met him there and trotted with him companionably. Stonnier considered her a friend. Some mornings she stayed with him past three or four properties, but this morning the collie next door came out and growled and she stopped at the line. *Yah* Stonnier growled back at the Collie and raised his elbow and jogged on.

After one spring thaw Stonnier dug a pit near the line close to McCoors's driveway. McCoors was quick to defend the integrity of his property. He had taken his neighbor on the other side to court on a right-of-way dispute. He asked Stonnier what he was doing.

He was going to bury dogshit.

"You don't have to do that here," McCoors said.

"It's your dog's," Stonnier said.

That afternoon a man from the Board of Health drove up to the house. Allan was down at The Fish & Chips watching them shingle the new roof. The man told Verna it was illegal to bury garbage. He told her about the hazard to the groundwater supply. He said the fine could be fifty dollars a day as long as the nuisance continued unabated. He left a red notice. This unsettled Verna, as she had always thought there were ways to work things out.

Allan went to the board and said they were off-base. A human being had to get a porcelain bowl and running water and an expensive piping system to get rid of his waste but a dog could leave it anywhere. It was off-base. The health officer said he didn't write the laws, he enforced them, and Allan better close the pit and not open another one. The newspaper carried a story under the headline PRIVATE DUMP OWNER THREATENED WITH FINE. Stonnier thought it gave the idea that he was trying to get away with something.

He wrote a letter to the editor. Melvin Brate didn't print it. He thought it was because Brate was still peeved about a previous letter he had written saying that the Otter River Bank was using the small type to sneak foreclosures over on people, trying to get out of the old low-interest rates into the new crazy rates. Stonnier knew about that because they had done it to his cousin. In his letter to the editor Stonnier gave the names of the man who ran the bank and the men who were on its investment committee and said that was no way for neighbors to act when they had signed their names to a contract. The bank was the biggest advertiser in the paper, so naturally Melvin Brate didn't print the letter. Allan couldn't understand that; reading the *Cape Cod Fog's* editorials on Free Speech Stonnier had the idea Brate wouldn't be afraid of a grizzly on a dark night. Allan got up at town meeting in Non-Agenda Time and read his bank letter to the voters to let them know what was going on. It was the first time he had ever gotten to his feet to talk to over a thousand people, and it was no harder than holding your hand in a fire.

Melvin Brate sat with his arms folded and looked hard at the floor while Alan spoke about his newspaper not saying anything on what the bank was doing. Brate had published just that day the editorial on "Your Free Press: Bastion of Liberty" that he counted on for an award from the League of Weekly Publishers, and here was this fried-clam peddler carrying on. Without dignifying the specific subject with additional publicity, the paper acknowledged Stonnier's two-minute bumble with an editorial that said private matters didn't belong either in newspapers or town meetings. So it wasn't surprising that Brate didn't print the dogshit-pit letter either even though Stonnier called it scat.

Verna was secretly glad they didn't. She thought there ought to be another way to go about it so the dog owners wouldn't get upset and more people wouldn't look at her sideways and stop going to The Fish & Chips. She knew there was no use saying that to Allan unless she could tell him another way that might work but she couldn't think of any. He had been such a usual man when she married him and people were getting the idea he was an oddball. She couldn't clearly see why that was because he had a right to take it up about the dogs, but nevertheless he ought to do it a different way for his own sake and not write to the proper paper or take it up at town meeting. It irritated people.

One day Stonnier counted eighteen dogs at the juncture of his lane and the Association road.

The Association road went into the blacktop that wound and rolled toward the town. The houses on either side were on the required acres and fully suited to their purposes. Once

home to cranberry farmers, fuel dealers, printers, boat builders, lobstermen—Stonnier knew the names that went with
the oldest properties—they had been bid away by retirement
and stock-market bankrolls at stiff prices in the sixties, terrible prices in the eighties and the biggest number you would
guess after the depression of the nineties. The new owners
had the means to dormer up and lay on wings and garages.
On some properties two and three houses stood where before
there had been a low shingle house, a big garden and woods.
The newcomers followed the traditional styles of Chatham
Road rendered for art shows on the high-school green—salt
boxes, houses, houses-and-a-half; a Greek revival presented
its masonic profile: well-shrubbed, fenced. One ghost of
gnawed and mossy shingles had withstood all tenders to pur-
chase and a siege of trumpet vines, rampant lilacs and fattening cedars intent on taking it down.

Only the jolly gold-and-blue French house looked as
though it ought to have been in the old town where there
were other houses of the style built by managers of the company that laid the telephone cable to France; indeed it had
been trucked from town in the deal with the architectural
commission that licensed the Cable Station Model to be built.
To Stonnier the French house coming down Chatham Road at
two miles an hour with outriders from the telephone company and the electric company and the police was the most
memorable event since the passage of the great glacier, which
he had not witnessed. Had he not come into money so late,
or had he thought about it earlier, this would have been the
house Stonnier would have built for his family. The French
house sat square on the ground and knew how to shed water
off its hat. It looked like a toby jug; not only was it gold and
blue, but its cornice was striped with purple and the door was
gunpowder red.

"It's different," he responded to Verna who thought it was a
rather queer house that would fit in better if it were white.
"You just like things one way or another. People see things
differently."

He liked the moment of coming out on the blacktop around the corner from West Bay and finding himself two weeks further into spring, jogging by the French house with the long hedge of breaking forsythia skirted with daffodils. The air here stank of dog too. Some of it was spring rot coming out of the ground. Most of it was dog.

Ahead on the long straight stretch Gordon's basset—that dog must be a hundred years old—carrying his skin like a soaked blanket, turned and turned in the middle of the road trying to find a way to let his sub-luxated rear end down and create the right precedent for the rest of him. He slept there every morning for an hour or two unless the snow was a foot deep. Regular drivers knew to watch for him, and the Lord protected Sam the basset against everybody else. That dog was going to get it one day. The driver that did it better have a good head start and not ask around whose dog it was so he could tell them he was sorry but he had passed a car and there the dog was, in the middle of the road, and he had done his best to avoid him, he was sorry, he knew what it was to lose a dog, he had two himself, don't shoot, please don't shoot. You couldn't know anymore what to expect if there was a dog in it. Juries looked at those dog people out there. If you ran for sheriff you took questions at public meetings and the dog people heard your answers. Senators wanted some of that DOG-PAC money, especially because the DOG-PAC people said what they were really interested in wasn't dogs but good government. If there was a dog question coming up at town meeting you saw people there to vote you never saw anywhere else. They went home after the vote and left the rest to find a quorum for the payroll and potholes.

Allan Stonnier was the only human being afoot on Chatham Road. His red sweatshirt was well known at this hour. Most of the sparse traffic was pickups with elbows crooked out the windows, wheels crunching and kicking up cans, wrappers, cups laid down by the pickups that had gone that way earlier, tools and dogs riding behind. Allan saw the green BusterBoy with the sunburst on the radiator that made it Dexter Reddick's. Without being too obvious Stonnier adjusted course to the edge of the road. He couldn't be absolutely sure Reddick wouldn't take a swerve at him for the hell of it. He prepared to break from the shoulder for the grass slope. Reddick went by with angry eyes, threw up a finger. Reflexively, Stonnier gave it back. He heard the BusterBoy braked hard behind him and pushed hard in reverse as it came back. He had it in view over his shoulder and kept going. Reddick passed, got twenty feet beyond and put his head out the window.

"What did I see you do?"

"The same as you." By then he was past the truck and Reddick had to grind back again to talk to him.

"Let me see you do that again you fuckhead. You old fart. You can't get it up. You firebug. I'll burn your ass." Stonnier kept going. Reddick jack-started a groove in the blacktop and went on his way. Stonnier decided to take the side road that went toward the dump.

Pillard's pack of huskies that he had brought back from Alaska last year saw him coming and started their manic racket. Pilliard had one-upped everybody at The Landing Bar with that one. Jesus, twelve huskies, did you ever see such dogs? You could hide your arm in the fur. The strut and drive of those legs. They had Chinese faces like they were people. Those people fucked their dogs. Pilliard had them in the cyclone-fenced stockade he put up to hold his cords when he had been in the stove-wood business. Ten feet high and ground area about as big as any factory you would find in a place like Cape Cod, lots of room even for twelve huskies.

Pilliard's idea was to take them to fairs and show them for a good price, pulling a sled he fitted with siliconed nylon runners that slipped over turf. Take your picture with a real team of Eskimo huskies. Children's birthday parties. Beats ponies all hollow. Fourth of July parades. He brought Santa Claus to The 1776 Mall. Altogether only a dozen brief outings all year. The dogs were used to doing miles of work in cold weather. In the stockade they hung around. At night they could be heard barking for hours for their own reasons, and the sound carried to West Bay.

Verna thought Allan must be running on the dump road because he would be there about now and there went Pilliard's huskies. They didn't often see people go by on foot. They acknowledged pedestrians and slow drivers by lunging at the fence, climbing, piling on, snarling, yelping powerfully. Allan had driven her by and slowed the car so she could hear it up close. It scared her. It was more like mad screaming than barking, all of them exciting each other. There were some things Verna wished Allan didn't do, and one of them was running past Pilliard's huskies.

"Run someplace else," Pilliard said. "You don't like dogs and they know it and they don't like you so why the fuck don't you run someplace else?"

It was no use explaining to a man who didn't already know it that it was a public road and he was there before the dogs anyhow. And even if he wasn't.

Stonnier left them yelping, went over the crest of the rise and around the next corner, running, feeling good, well sweated as he went toward halfway. It was the dumb part of the route, the old mall, The Mall and The 1776 Mall, and the file of flat-roofed taxpayers and show-windowed front porches of Old Downtown; service stations, eating places, clothes shops, music stores, cleaners, laundries, drugstores elbowing to be seen along the bypassed highway number.

He could have gone around by the marsh road and avoided town, but there was one thing to be said for Main Street, it smelled better than anywhere else. Better than West Bay behind the dunes where the ocean first lost its innocence; better than Chatham Road and all the lived-on lanes and roads from the bridge to Province Lands. He had never thought to live to the day when downtown smelled better than the countryside. The merchants saw to it. You couldn't let a leashed dog step onto one of those neat rectangles of shrubbery if you didn't want a ticket. If a stray wandered into the old mall, The Mall or The 1776, the Small Animal Officer

showed up fast and snared him into the cage mounted on his
Lesser Aunt Tilly Blast-Off. If a dog hunched to empty out
you had to drag him to the library lawn. Even the dog people
understood the deal. You left the merchants alone, they left
you alone.

That soon after dawn Old Downtown could have been a
movie set in storage. Cars and service trucks of early risers
were parked in front of Annie O who opened first for the
fishermen. The overnight lights in the stores and the street-
lights watched him go by. Stanchions of sulfur light guarded
the plaza of Canine City, with its eleven veterinarians, four
cosmetologists, several outfitters; the portrait studio featured
the work of fifteen internationally-known dog artists; an
architect displayed model residences: Cape, half-Cape, Federal, Victorian, Bauwowhaus, duplex, ranch.

The stoplight turned irrationally against him, as if pro-
grammed to recognize a man of ordinary size in a red sweatshirt running in from the west. Wind batted through the open
cross-street and went back again behind the solid buffer of
storefronts until it came to the empty lot on the cove where
The Fish & Chips had been. He faced into it, running in
place, when he got there. The real-estate people never
stopped bringing him offers. He was going to leave that up to
his children to decide. The land was money in the bank.
"That's what everybody needs, Verna, something in back of
him so no matter how hard he's pushed he doesn't have to
give in to others. That's what it's all about. More people could
be like that if they didn't want too much."

The Conservation Commission asked, if he wasn't going
to use it, would he consider deeding it to them for the honor
of his name in Melvin Brate's paper and the tax deduction.
They thought a price might be worked out if he met them
halfway. He thought about it. He got as far as thinking what
kind of sign he would require them to put up if he sold them
the land but he could never get the wording right enough to
ask if they would do it. He knew if he got it right they
wouldn't. He neatened up the section of burned-out foun-

dation the building inspector allowed and let the lot sit there with the sign.

They stole the sign the first night. He wasn't going to fool with them, he went right to a concrete monument anchored with bent iron rods into a six-foot square concrete pad. They tried to jump it out with a chain but it would have taken a dozer and they never got around to that. They hit it with a hammer now and then. They painted out the inscription. He used to go back a few times a year to put it in shape but he hadn't had to touch it for two years now. The old generations had lost interest, and it didn't mean that much even to the young Reddicks unless something happened to stir them up.

Coming on their first glimpse of saltwater in twenty miles visitors swung onto the apron and reached for their cameras. Alert to station their wives for the photo opportunity where George Washington watered his horses and the saltwater beyond, they walked over to read the legend:

SITE OF THE FISH & CHIPS RESTAURANT
BURNED DOWN BY VANDALS A.D. 2002
IN HONOR OF THEIR DOGS

They threw up their hands. What's that all about? Stonnier himself wasn't satisfied with the statement but after so many years the whole story was boring to anybody but himself anyhow.

He had kept a dozen clipped mallards for his own table in a chicken-wire pen half in and half out of the water, the way you penned ducks if you had a waterfront. There had been a terrible squawking, and when he looked out from the kitchen door the two dogs that patrolled Reddick's garage at night were running wild in the pen breaking wings and necks, tossing every duck they could get their jaws on. He hollered at them but you couldn't call a dog off anything like that. He got his shotgun and came out and drove a charge into the side of one and the other ran off and Reddick came over from his garage goddamming him.

It got in the paper that Reddick was there to get his dogs and Stonnier threatened him with the gun to keep him off and he shot the dog.

A week later a southerly breeze pulled an early morning fire out of the rubbish trailer onto the shingle. Flame was all through The Fish & Chips by the time the pumper got there. His was the fourth restaurant that went up that fall, and the arson investigator from the state asked him how his business had been. They went over his deposits at the bank. The insurance company took two years to pay up.

He ran where he stood while he looked around and checked out the site. It was as usual. The fresh northeaster gusted at him out of a mist that lay up to the land at the water's edge. A gull stalked the tidal drain looking for garbage. Another, unseen, cried as if lost. On the scrim of fog appeared the shed of The Fish & Chips with the huge lobster standing guard and then The Fish & Chips with the new Cape Cod roof and the kitchen wing. He looked out the back window and saw Reddick's dogs in the pen and went after them. A charred beam leaned on a course of cement block that had been the foundation. Ravined and grainy, the blacktop was being worked by frost and the roots of locust and wild cherry. Spindly cedars had found footing. He remembered when they had poured the blacktop; four inches and four of gravel under it and then ocean sand, and the cedars had found enough to grow on down there. He felt himself already cooling out and took off at a 120 jog back through town, wiping sweat from his forehead with the flat of his hand.

The last thing he discussed with himself as he went up the rise at the mall and turned again toward Pilliard's (he had intended to go back by the road around the marsh but forgot it in the intensity of the discussion) was how his daughter and her children could be made to keep their minds on being positioned so they never had to give in to others. All he could do was leave them the land, they had to understand what it was for. If they sold it they would have the money and if you had money you had all kinds of duties to it. You had to see that you didn't lose any of it and you had to get the best interest for it and you bought things you didn't need that brought you new duties, like a place in Florida. The land would stay there to back you up. He didn't stop thinking about that until he got into range of Pilliard's huskies and they started in on him again. Pilliard was carrying an armful of pipe, fence posts maybe, and spat a word at him he couldn't hear. He kept going.

The wind off the bay blew some of the sound away but she heard the pack distinctly again. She threw the last intended handful of cracked corn for the quail and jays and listened. She wore untied walking shoes for slippers and a nubby white robe over her nightgown. She had brushed her hair but not in detail and its style was a simple black-speckled gray flare cut off at her earlobe. She took her wristwatch out of the robe pocket but couldn't read it. Her glasses were still inside on the table. If that was Allan he would be nine or ten minutes. Then he would shower and she would be dressed and have breakfast on. It wasn't an egg day. He might want tuna on toast.

The dogs went on. She wasn't dressed to stay out but the dogs were going on. She picked up a dead branch, carefully positioned it and flicked a turd into the rough. All the turds over which oak leaves had settled stirred and gave off a tribal odor as if they were a single living thing giving warning. She threw another handful of corn without noticing very exactly what she was doing. Pilliard's dogs sounded louder but that couldn't be. They were where they were. In the tops of the scratch pines the wind had not changed. Individual voices could be distinguished rising out of the wild yammer of the pack.

Were Pilliard's dogs out? He leashed and ran them sometime in the back of the dump, but that was farther not nearer, and never this early. She felt nervous and wished to know something. She started toward the house to look up Pilliard's name in the book and telephone him but knew immediately that was not the thing to do. The thing to do was to get in the car and drive over there.

She was not constrained now by any civilized notion that she should not be seen, even by herself, to overreact. She wished to act as quickly and as arbitrarily as she knew how and get over to the dump road. The Ford spurted back out of the garage, skidded while she pulled on the wheel to get it around, and went out the lane faster than McCoors's dogs had ever seen it come at them, they couldn't believe it was going that fast until it kicked the big kind-of-Airedale into the ditch. She had no time to regret or succor and pushed the gas harder. The wheels jumped out of potholes and ruts clawing air and jolted down. She was frightened by her speed. She held on as if it were out of her control. Coming to the fork at the blacktop she judged—willed, rather—that she could beat the blue car, and cut it off. Its horn lectured her past Sam the Bassett sitting on the stripe with his back to her, knowing she wouldn't dare, until she lost it at the turn beyond the straightaway.

A quarter-mile up toward Pilliard's she saw them on the road. She looked for a human figure but there was only the pack and whatever it was they were larking around on the road. She kept her hand on the horn and drove at them not thinking any longer that it was possible he had gone another way or got up a tree or even into Pilliard's house. She put the pedal on the floor. She was angry at Allan for getting himself into anything like this. He could have lived his life like other people. But he hadn't and that's how it was and, enraged, she owed him as many of them as she could get her wheels into.

Yellow Jackets

1

THE path up from the water is steep and I naturally kept my head down when climbing and—as often as I had been back and forth—it could have been weeks since I looked at that side of my house. I wouldn't have looked then if I hadn't stopped to kick a branch aside and, being stopped, happened to glance up. *Teddy Roosevelt*.

I see faces in stones and floor vinyl, no great gift, you probably do too. If all the constellations weren't used up and I had the interest I could see mythic figures in the stars. I don't see in a creative way as Michelangelo saw a figure in a block of marble or Borglum saw the faces of presidents waiting to be blasted out of the Black Hills cliffs. I don't change anything in the object. It changes me.

I got a small charge of pleasure to see my house come out of the wooded hill as from a cave, a prehistoric Teddy Roosevelt kind of square-jawed *thing* with stiles of the balcony railing for teeth and multiple-window eyes staring through the sun to the town across the bay.

My pleasure was interrupted by a puzzle: what were the spots the size of coins scattered along the foot-wide facia of the balcony's footing edge? I had gone to the lumberyard myself and chosen the boards one by one, turning over the stacked lumber, sighting the true of the edges, putting aside wavering, marbled and knotty lengths. I had paid a price I would never forget for clear stock and couldn't have failed to notice knots. I looked closer.

They were not knots, they were knotholes the size of nickels and dimes. I kept thinking *knots* and *knotholes* because I couldn't think of anything else, but I knew there had been no knots in that wood.

The holes varied slightly in size. They were cleanly bored and rather uniformly round. They were—whoa! what's going on!—bullet holes!

Instinct took hold. I ducked to protect my neck as I swung around in reconnoiter mode to see where rifle shots might have come from. My wife and baby were inside that house. Who would walk the shoreline or sit out there in a boat and plink at it? Forget plink—this was heavy stuff, .30-.30 maybe.

Three small craft idled in mid-channel. Vehicles, at this distance the size of Zig-Zag Cracker Jack prizes, were parked at the town landing on the far shore. Gulls snacked the tide for something to hold them until dinner. The scene lazed in the benevolent light and silence of a Sunday afternoon in August on Cape Cod.

I kept thinking *bullets* but I didn't believe *bullets* anymore than I believed *knots*. All I knew was this amazing phenomenon of *holes* materializing on my new house—overnight, as far as I knew. I counted seventeen holes the size of small change in the narrow house-length strip. They were not all as neatly round as I had first seen them to be. Some were oval. Some had been bored at slight angles. Every hole was in the facia, not one above or below. Not a window shot out.

"Paula!" I hollered. She opened the balcony door. "Did you ever notice any holes in this facia board?"

She wasn't sure what a facia board was. She bent over the railing to see what I was talking about.

"We have holes all across here. Come on down a minute. Bring the binocs."

The deck—they call everything walked-on around here a deck—gave me particular satisfaction as I had pushed the builder all the way to get it right. I wanted it the full-length, not just off the dining alcove. I didn't want it supported by posts. I wanted the two-by-ten joists that underlay the upper floor cantilevered as far as prudent engineering allowed, and a marine-plywood deck laid down. The builder said we could go out five feet without danger of sag if we didn't put a piano on it.

I didn't want the joists exposed; where they pierced the wall the house would be disarmed against northeasters. I accepted the cost to sheet the underside of the joists and seal the beam-ends with the board.

Paula had been born and raised on Cape Cod and never heard of holes in houses except from red squirrels and woodpeckers; these holes were too small, too neat. I speculated with her again about knots and bullets. I arced the binoculars slowly across the view and didn't see anything out there that had anything to do with these holes. No, I didn't believe bullets made them, but I was a father and had to express a responsibility I didn't know how to deal with right then: "Where's Ruth?"

She was in her playpen.

"Let's keep an extra eye on her until we figure what this is all about."

While we discussed the mystery a bumblebee big enough to saddle came out of nowhere, fastened onto the board, staggered toward a hole and heaved itself in. At the same time, another bumbler, looking like it was hauling itself around in a black-and-yellow sack, lurched from a hole and flew off.

Next morning I was in at the opening of Minute Man Hardware to consult with Bill, who would know. Bill had heard about something called carpenter bees when he lived in New Jersey but had never seen them with his own eyes and had never heard of them around here. He suggested a call to the Ag Office in Barnstable. The Ag Office never heard of carpenter bees and gave me the number of Mahlon Neere, a beekeeper.

Neere had never heard of carpenter bees. He knew about carpenter ants—

"Friend, you can put your index finger in these holes. No ant is going to make a hole like that."

"You betcha," Neere said. "I was just going to say no ant is going to make a hole like that."

I went back to Minute Man and bought the last bottle of a liquid so mean that the federal government said no more could be sold after the first of next month; except for export. The canal that separated us from the mainland didn't qualify Cape Codders for this benefit that could be experienced routinely in Upper Volta. So much for American citizenship.

"What are you going to do?" Paula asked when she saw the bottle and the look on my face. She wouldn't allow me to shoot squirrels within her hearing. The first day we moved in she put out bird feeders. She bought traps made like cages so I could carry mice to the dump and let them loose. She was a member of the Association for the Preservation of Cape Cod that issued pamphlets on dangers from pesticides. So was I.

"Drown them," I said.

"You're going to poison them."

"You betcha. They're eating your house."

"Bumblebees don't sting."

"You're not listening. They're eating your house."

I took an old shirttail out of the rag bag and a scissors and the dire stuff from Minute Man, and a throwaway pie plate to pour it in, and went outside. I cut the cloth into bacon-strip lengths, dipped the strips in the liquid that stank of malevolence—*lump that about dilution*—and with a stick poked the rags into the holes.

Dinner conversation ran to short sentences. My subjects were shot down with *No, Maybe* and *We'll see*. We communicated more elaborately than usual with the baby, urging one more one-more-spoonful, arguing the counter-productivity of throwing things on the floor.

"How are we going to feed ourself if we keep throwing our spoon on the floor?" Paula asked.

Having a child to look after raised a grain of archness in Paula I had not known was there. I forgave her. Mothering can upset all kinds of metabolism, including the linguistic. I offset her with what I supposed the child at some level would assimilate as a dryer manner if I kept pushing it.

"Let's shape up on that. Chinese kids are starving. We've discussed that before. We keep going over the same ground. Eat."

Without taking her eyes from the face issuing the words, she accepted the spoon recharged with supper, held it in her fist poised to fire at her ear, her hair or (her intelligent eyes promised) her mouth. To have an intelligent child is pleasing. At the same time a lively imagination provokes anxiety that experimental choices may be made that parents know are simply no good. She flung the spoon from her, slumped as deeply as she could against the strap that cinched her in place and began to kick the air. I cleaned up the muck.

Joining Paula in the ordeal of parenting reduced my offense against nature from a divorcing to a brooding issue. It became settled that Ruth (I resisted Ruthie) might dine later. For now, she would continue to pedal her invisible road, while her mother did the dishes and her father went outside to see what might be going on with his bee trap.

No carpenter bees were around. The evening was serene. The rag blockades were doing their assigned task.

I became aware of thrumming within the sealed space. With awareness, the volume of sound increased. I imagined thousands of fluttering wings, and tiny voices petitioning me. I felt sympathy and guilt but life is notorious for casting up rotten choices and I didn't know how I could have done it a better way. They had eaten their way in, they could eat their way out. The playing field was level.

While I indulged this honorable reverie one of the rags trembled. It was being manipulated. It was being pushed out. It was dislodged and fell to the ground, and a bee heaved itself to the lip of the hole and sprang off in apparent bonny health.

"Good for you," I thought when I got over my astonishment.

I watched another plug shoved aside and again one bee escaped.

"Paula!" I hollered. "Come out here. You won't believe this."

By the next morning five cloth strips, stiffened in their drying maximum poison, lay on the ground. No bees were seen or heard.

I drilled the holes to a uniform size, cut dowels and drove them home. I stained them to match the rest of the board.

Occasionally thereafter we saw what everybody called bumblebees but we never again saw them act like carpenter bees, although friends from New Jersey said they were known down there, the varnished black abdomens of carpenters distinguishing them from furry-bellied bumblers. We never knew whether hundreds were entombed in the deck or whether all had flown to a more hospitable environment or whether there ever had been any more.

I came out of that experience as probably Cape Cod's only living authority on carpenter bees. Not bad for a guy who had been raised in the city and been a high-school history teacher until four years ago.

2

Two stories high on the water side, at its entrance the house was (it still is) a single floor with a tilted view that had been stripped of trees and skinned back a few degrees. The dirt sliced off the hill made a platform for the foundation.

The land lay so precipitously that the building inspector said if we didn't want a house full of water someday I better lay up a stiff wall to divert storm runoff aside into the woods. Through clay and stony rubble that we envisioned one day would be a tapestry of plantings, a curving stair of railroad ties came down from the road, around the building inspector's railroad tie wall to a weedling terrace at the door. A more level right-of-way had been bulldozed across neighboring land to bring in the contractor's equipment but it was too rutty and rooty for the family car and the pickup. Hardening the road was a project for next spring. In the meantime we parked "upstairs" on the county road, and Paula recited to herself what accidents to prepare against before she ventured into the descent with Ruth.

In the first big winter rain, water coursed down the slope, scalped sand and yellow clay off the rocks and wore ruts deep enough to found a famous river in. It spat through the joints of the wall and dribbled down its face to the terrace. Paula didn't like the looks of it. I said it was supposed to happen that way. The sandy ground under the terrace would absorb the dribbled water. If the wall were masonry-tight, water-pressure would in time take it down. Those were words I had heard said. I had no absolute confidence in any of it after I said it too. Reality might be different. I put on oilskins and boots and went out to shovel gutters to encourage a more rapid runoff into the woods.

Rain kept coming. It gathered behind the wall and over-flowed to the terrace in a majestic, pleated shantung-silk cur-tain eighty feet wide. While we watched dumbfounded and helpless through the big window, the flood pooled, over-whelmed my gutters, rose to the step, rose to the sill of the door. Then the rain stopped. Within an hour the pool on the terrace disappeared into the sandy bottom, leaving a forlorn stand of muddied young grass. On the hill, boulders bald as the skulls of idols emerged to look around.

I didn't want to see a niagara pour over the top of that wall and rise to our doorsill again. The trees that had been taken off the hill were still piled in the side lot. I chain-sawed them into lengths I could handle and scattered the logs down the grade in a pattern that worked a carny game on the next storm, fooled it into dissipating a little stream here, a little stream there, always trending to the sides. The next down-pour didn't gather into rivers and didn't overflow the wall. *Yes, good thinking for a city boy who had been a Cape Codder hardly five years.*

When spring came we accelerated our planting scheme. I

dug leaf rot from the woods and piled it behind the logs; dug
bayberry, rugosa roses and young cedars from the shoreline,
hauled them up the path and set them in the sand and leaf
rot; dug overgrown clumps from my father-in-law's day-lily
bed and brought mosses from the woods.

Until that year I had thought privately that if I wanted to
live on the Cape I might have been wiser to transfer my
teaching credentials. I hadn't known much about business.
My father-in-law had a paint store and felt at his fingertips
the growing tide of people buying houses and fixing up their
properties. He told me about the fence franchise and encouraged me.

Leaving a secure job had not been exactly true to my style.
In the old days when I played dormitory poker the others
kidded me for folding if I didn't have the cards. The joke was
that when the dealer was asked "What's the game?" some
called *Five-card Stud*, some called *Treys Wild* and Dick Sterko's
game was *Patience*. I grinned and bore it. I won a little more
often than I lost. Maybe they had more fun, I don't know. I
was comfortable with my game.

To get the fence business going had used up more checks
than I liked to write, but now I began to make some real
money.

I bought the plants Paula named from the nursery and the
mail-order catalogs. I set firethorn, alyssum, artemesia, chry-
santhemums, heathers.

Straightening my back to rest from planting I placed a foot
on an idol's skull; I felt godlike myself, looking down the
landscaped hillside to my wall and my redwood furniture on
the terrace, my house weathering into the landscape. I
breathed air of celestial purity. I thought I had been dealt a
hand many others would have played worse.

There I was stung by a yellow-jacket wasp, a hardly noticed
match head dying on my arm. I brushed it, felt the writhing
fur justly impaled on its own anger.

Another buttoned on my ankle, and another on my neck
set off a brass alarm. I saw a dozen hover, guessed wildly

they must be in my hair, on my collar. I flailed like Lincoln's preacher who fought bees and slammed down the hill, insulting my father-in-law's lilies to their roots, took the wall at a jump and brought a few with me into the house behind the slammed door, hollering,

"Get in a bedroom with the baby and don't come out till I tell you!" I slammed the bathroom door behind me. I called out an explanation. "I may have brought some yellow jackets into the house. Stay put till I have a chance to check it out."

I went into the shower with my clothes on, stripped, found two of them to squash, threw my clothes out the window in case there were more. The scuffling and exclamations came through to Paula as Jacob wrestling with the angel. I opened the door carefully, put on a robe and looked around.

"I guess it's okay to come out," I said, feeling a little foolish, and chagrined to have put my family in harm's way for a couple of stings. "I wouldn't have come in the house with them if I'd thought."

"Look at me," Paula said. "Your face is swollen."

"They didn't sting me there. They got me on the arm and neck. And here." I showed her rosettes on my ankle and arm and where I supposed one was on my neck.

"Your face is swollen fat."

I had been out in the sun all afternoon. "It might be the sun."

My fingers felt stuffed, my forehead stretched. When I touched a finger to my forehead the surfaces met a leather scrim sooner than I expected. I saw my cheeks. My eyes were heavy. I felt woozy.

"I think I'll lie down," I said.

"No you won't. You'll get to Dr Fettig as fast as you can and if he isn't in we'll keep going to MedCenter. Come on, Ruthy, we're going for a ride with Daddy."

In that way I learned I was among the elect—elect as all who have peculiar vision, all who have extraordinary gifts not of their choosing; artists and accountants, extrasensory perceivers, mystics, idiot savants, dowsers; elect as magnets are to find the pole and Spanish Bourbons to die from scratches. If I didn't have handy the anti-venom kit Dr Fettig prescribed I could die when—pick a number—six yellow jacket wasps decided. A half-dozen yellow matches struck in the flare of azaleas and crackle of firethorn and Dick Sterko could be a goner.

I read up on them. Their name is *vespula*, species *vulgaris*, of the order *hymenoptera*. They are carnivores, tempted by the dead meat of mice, insects and, arguably, me. They are not without charm: inside their nests the young perk up like birds to get a malaxated ration. Best of all, they all die every year, all except the fertile queens.

They prefer ground nests under logs, stones and patches of moss, so I knew not to look for them in sultan hats hanging from branches or in mud flutes pasted under the eaves. Those were for hornets. I was wary enough of hornets and took them out of play when I encountered them shopping in the flowers or walking on the windows, but the wasps that issued from the ground, ill-tempered, camouflaged in the low growth, were my mortal enemy.

Stalking their erratic flight at a cautious distance, I waited for one to disclose the home of many. They wandered the day like truant boys without purpose. One might walk around on a leaf, fly to a twig, then bob around awhile in the air thinking of another idle way to kill time until he was expected home. They refused to show me where that home was.

I adjusted my habits to theirs. When I did my garden chores, I put on my Minute Man peaked cap, tucked my trousers into my shoes, buttoned the sleeves and collar of my shirt. I plunged my hands in branchy places de-li-cate-ly, kept an eye out when I reached the hoe to scratch the roots of crabgrass to the sun or scarify the varnish of the drying rain. When they approached to look me over with carnivorous speculations I stood quietly until their childish attention turned elsewhere.

Not until the summer nearly ended did I find them streaming in and out of a hole under a cap of moss. I had been at the spot a hundred times and not suspected the nest. I backed off. I got out the carpenter-bee elixir, saturated a rag, picked it up with the end of the hoe handle, and waited, holding the thready traffic in view while the sun settled toward set and I judged they were bivouacked for the night.

I approached the arena with caution. I rammed the morbid flag into the hole. With the extended handle I prodded the cloth into a tighter bundle, rammed it again and again and ran.

From the wall, ready to jump down and get the cover of the house, I kept the rag in my binoculars. I had not got them all. A few latecomers, back from scaring eagles, puzzled at the barricade, muttering my name. I imagined *ruin! ruin!* cried in the lair under the moss. In a frenzy—lumbering, carnivorous, stammering in slow camera frames on my glass—the late ones tried to tear their way in to the others. It became too dark. I went inside.

In the morning no yellow jackets were around. I put a spade in the ground and turned up the nest. They lay in masses.

Next year they were back, born of other queens, not in the poisoned nest but never far. They entered ivy, did not reappear; left spoors in midair, dwindled into motes, vanished, reappeared on their truant rounds. I did not find a nest again. I became accustomed to living with them, although mindful of their imminence as I planted and weeded the slope into the tapestry the Garden Club asked to show on the Summer Caravan.

The terrace I defended as my own. When yellow jackets invited themselves to Sterko's barbecue to feast on roasted meat and pecan rolls, I swatted them with magazines, blasted them with aerosol, trapped them under pastry domes, in butterfly nets.

As time passed and I remained unstung I treated them as familiars. Though I did not challenge them I waved them off without concern; named a fat one Mao Tse Sting and another for a cousin who sued his own sister.

The driveway on the right-of-way settled and hardened and came to a garage under a new wing of the house. It became a common lane for neighbors who ventured to build on the slope first assayed by Richard and Paula Sterko. An association was formed to pay for winter snowplowing and spring pothole-filling. Their dogs visited us. Richard Junior was born.

Ruth, now verging on being a young lady, in skinny-jeans, mouth fenced with wires, teeth strewn with ritual ornaments, veiled as a begum behind hair astray, stepped out the door to the terrace. She called something I did not hear clearly and before I could ask *Come again?* she decided to carry her question to me. As the stairs were too long around, she vaulted to a seat on top of the wall and came up the hill in a game of giant-strides.

Stunned by the marvelous justice of her advance that avoided every weed and seemed not to miss a catalog number, I finally got out the word to make her watch where she put her feet. "No!"

"Mother isn't home—" she said at the same time. She stopped. Daughters don't come to fathers for *No's*.

"I know your mother isn't home. She went to the dentist and took Rick with her. Now be careful where you walk. You're standing on a heather."

She then saw my meaning, bent down to repair the damage—and they rose around her.

I saw them before she did. "Stay!" I ordered, as to a dog, while I got my wits together. I came down to within arm's reach and motioned for her not to move from her crouch. I didn't know whether it might have been better to say *Run!* but I was committed to *Stay!* and dreaded that I had chosen wrong. The moment of choice had passed. She held like statuary and looked through the veil of hair for instruction. Fathers were for that.

I hollered "Help! Help! Somebody! Help!" into the void

surburban universe and said quietly to her, "Don't do anything to excite them. Breathe slowly. Move slowly. Try standing up very slowly. Tell me if you get a sting. It isn't much—
just a pinprick." I hollered again, "Help! Help! Help!"

As she rose, pretending the stillness of landscape, they rose
with her, issuing from the womb under the heather. I held
out my hand to draw them, to be quilted in with her where I
had condemned her to stand. They veered from the current
of my gesture.

"Sting," she said. "Knee."

"Hang in there. Let me know. If you get too many we'll run
for it. Try to wait them out."

I called again for help. I had stood here on the head of a
stone idol feeling like a god, and I knew now what a small
thing it was to be a god. Gods could do nothing about anything this dervish and immense. Gods decided that the game
was Wasps & Girls and set them down on earth, but didn't
know any better than anyone else whether the play should be
Stay! or *Run!*

I remembered with shame that I had not bothered to find
out if Ruth had inherited my flawed chemistry. There was
probably a test and I hadn't asked. I hadn't gotten a new anti-
venom kit when the date on the first one staled. I did not
even know where it was—in the medicine cabinet? In the
refrigerator? In the travel case from five years before when we
went to Williamsburg? I could reach out to her—to do nothing. I could not change places, mightily as I wished to. I
offered my hand again to the wasps. They rejected me.

I thought I had never loved anyone—not even Paula, not
even this child—as I loved her at this moment. I had given her
life and put her in the way of death. I did not pray. I was not a
praying man. I could imagine a god who had made the rules
but not one who would change them. The game I knew to
play was Patience.

"Leg," she said. She sniffled and tossed her head to shake
the veil of hair from her eye.

"Don't move. Stick it out. Let them lose interest and scatter." If they would be so accommodating.

My duty was plain enough: to run—to get to a phone and call the Rescue Squad, call the fire department—they knew how to inch boys out of chimneys, they must know about wasps; call Dr Fettig to bring the newest science. I could not leave her. Men whose companions die in lakes and under desert sun are thought of with a touch of curiosity, something Dreiser's young American did not foresee. The men in Donner's camp who said goodbye to women in the snow, going for help, the way more harsh, yet toward a kinder land, faltered lest reckoned benefit appear the felon's part—they went anyhow; but heroes like myself, of the second class, are called up by the neural recollection that admiration for some kinds of survivors is alloyed. I could not leave her. I called out again and was answered.

"Hey, Sterko, what's the problem?"

The voice came from behind, from the hilltop road. Nate Harris, who worked for the telephone company and had one of the new houses, had heard me. Nate couldn't see anything wrong; just Sterko and his girl standing and looking at each other.

"Nate—get the Rescue Squad. We're trapped by yellow jackets. We can't move. Tell them we're allergic. Bring wasp venom. She has already been stung. It can be fatal if they don't get here fast. Fast, Nate."

"Roger. I'll get right back to you." The plaid shirt and the long face, a vase for the stiff shock of black hair, disappeared.

I reassured her. "Hang in there. They'll be here soon." I put a number on it, as if I knew. "A couple of minutes."

Wasps crawled on her. They sewed her in with insane needlework. I coached her. "You don't want to excite them. Stay steady. I don't know if you're allergic. I don't think you are. Your face isn't swollen. If you were allergic your face would be swollen."

She said through unmoving lips. "You're allergic. Get away."

"That's okay. Be quiet."

Vincent and Carole Rorrock came around the garage to the terrace. "Was that you called for help?"

I told them what was happening. Vincent looked along the wall and went for the hose coiled on its drum at the faucet. "What if I turn a hose on them? It might drive them off."

"I don't know. It might excite them. I don't want to excite them."

"Just a light mist maybe."

"Don't you do anything with that hose," Carole said. "You don't know. If it was me I'd turn it on as hard as I could if I wanted to drive them off."

Heavy, light—it was vocabulary. Problems at a distance—war, peace, poverty, taxes, the sins of movie stars, the promises of legislators—yielded to the vocabulary of people standing around talking. My kinds of question were: Was George Washington a patriot or the servant of agrarian interests? Did western technology repel the Arab invasion or was it the inability of camels to subsist above a Mediterranean Mason-Dixon line? Failures of vocabulary had no consequences, seldom even chagrin after noticed error. Ruth and wasps were in front of me. Error had consequences. "Let's wait for the Rescue Squad," I said to Rorrock; and to Ruth, "How are you doing, kid?"

"Scared," she said, and looked it. "Four stings."

"It's okay to be scared. Hang in there. It won't be long."

"Right shoulder."

I could expect her to take only so much. Then I would have to say *Run for it!* and get her into the house, no matter what. How much was *only so much*?

A wild loopy signal burst in nearby and climbed the county road, warning everybody who survived the heart attack to get out of the way. It was too soon for the skirl of the Rescue ambulance; only on a still night with the wind right could it be heard starting from the fire department at the highway end of town. This would be a police cruiser that had been intercepted and told to get to Tarn Road and see what was going on.

Back on the top of the hill, Harris had his arm up to semaphore the cruiser. "Here comes a cop car. Squad's on the way." The cruiser hunted along the berm for the best place to pull in. The officer, a young man I didn't recognize, must be a summer man, got out with a leashed telephone in hand. He knew he was extremely important.

Harris said: "They're trapped by yellow jackets, officer. I phoned the Rescue Squad."

The information was too trivial to be acknowledged. The officer spoke confidentially to headquarters. The other side responded in manic squawks torn from the speaker's throat. When the conversation ended, the officer folded his arms, the phone still in his hand, crossed his legs, leaned against the car door and looked at us without comment. The leashed metal continued to glare around and exhale gases like a hampered minotaur.

From the direction of Head of Bay came the first joyful noise of the Rescue Squad, and a second baritone siren.

I turned to say it would *really* be two minutes — preposterously, she was grinning, showing her ornamented teeth. She blurted thinly, not to incend the wasps, "All I wanted was to find out if you knew where there are any stamps."

As the notion of stamps growing in the garden was so absurd, her grin expanded to laughter, not without tears, but at its core laughter, the shaking unmanageable laughter of a child.

My face had no choice but to mimic hers mirthlessly.

3

The ambulance drew up behind the cruiser. The pumper went on to the hydrant. The skirl wound down. In train were cars and pickups come for fire, blood or clangored metal wrapped around a telephone pole. All there was to it was a man and a girl down on the hillside looking at each other.

Brice Cahill, lead man of the Squad, rolled his stubby body out. He asked in his ordinary nasal whine of disbelief, "What have you got? Bees?"

"Yellow jackets. Have you got a venom kit?"

"We do. First we have to get you out of there. You allergic?"

"I am. I don't know about her. She's been stung. I haven't." It was a reproach. "How do you handle these things?"

"Mahlon Neere's coming with smoke if you can wait." It set her off again. *Smoke!* She saw herself as Joan of Arc. She imprisoned laughter as best she could. Cahill saw that she shook.

"You'll be all right, little girl. We're going to have you out of there in a cat's wink." *Cat's wink!* Hilarious.

"The little girl's been stung?"

"Five or six times."

"How are you doing, little girl?"

"Fine."

"What's her name?"

"Ruth."

"Ruthy, how would it be if we brought down a fire hose and blew the bees away while we helped you get up to the ambulance?" *Rorrock wasn't dumb. Neither was his wife. Only Dick Sterko the god was dumb.* "Do you think you can handle that, Ruthy?"

"Yes."

Cahill called down the road. "All right with the hose. Let's have it here. Deevers—" his aide—"you go down around the back of these good people so when the water hits you can push them up. We don't want to knock them down."

The firemen hauling a hose trashed the evergreen border and laid heavily booted feet in my garden. In the scale of events I knew I should not guide them to a better stand. Cahill instructed, "Open the spray up to about a three-foot circle and hit it right at them. You ready down there?"

They threw the water high till they got the diameter right, then hit us with it in discrete fat bullets of salvation. I grabbed her arm as we were shoved from behind and pushed to the top where other hands reached down to bring us the last yard. She laughed again and again as promptings of the bizarre struck her—these people rubbernecking, the cruiser's sapphire eye batting at her, the policeman's stagy impassivity amid chaos, wasps rejecting her father's offered hand, stamps growing in the garden. "There weren't—there weren't any in the desk." It was too comical.

"It'll sting a little bit," Cahill said as the medic pinched her arm for the needle.

Drenched, erect, shaking with laughter, she agreed, "Just what I need." She fainted to the ground.

Every family has a story. A small degree this way, it's an anecdote, a small degree another way and it may be recalled with profound sadness. I'm a lucky man to have only an anecdote.

Many times I've sat on the terrace and replayed the scene. If I had it to do again I would like to know if it were better *Run!* than *Stay!* but how can we know? I am sure you know because you weren't there.

I think about her laughter. In the end, for me it comes down to her laughter. At the moment my face benignly—vacuously perhaps—mimics my memory of hers I experience the purest joy.

Once when she brought the grandchildren to visit we sat out here and she asked how I was getting along with the wasps. I had never been stung again. I said, "I don't fool myself, though. They are my mortal enemy and may get me yet. But at one level I have"—there is not always a suitable word—"a fondness for them. I don't know whom or what but yellow jackets to thank for your laughter." It isn't quite dry enough for my taste and I never said it again till now.

Earthly Justice

1

AT first the words were in the wrong sequence to be heard, for death is slight news until a familiar name is in it. "Killed . . . Pittsburgh . . . *Sherroder!*"

Try it yourself. How much do you really care about people starving in Africa or sleeping on the sidewalks of Boston or being shot in their garages in Pittsburgh? You care, yes. You're human, and nothing is alien et cetera. But as if they were your own flesh and blood? No aunt of yours is in any of those fixes; not that you know of. Nothing happens that you care all that much about until you hear a name.

I was reading *The Black Arrow* and a half-listening to KDKA on the shortwave. I didn't hear anything until I heard the name of my father's sister.

Killed . . . Pittsburgh . . . Sherroder! *Aunt Leora!*

I held onto the book as to a brother in a scary place while the newscaster put it in order again for late-arriving minds (the way they used to before jobs were filled by people with no memory of how things should be done. Now they write for radio as if you were tuned from the first word, as if you had nothing to do but sit there and hear them tell the story from A to Z. If you miss the name of the country where the airplane went down in the first sentence, they never tell you again.)

"The dead woman's husband, Dr Myron Sherroder, a well-known Pittsburgh physician, was at home at the time—"

The young don't often play a part as large as being the first to know. I burst out of my room and went down the stairs shouting, "Aunt Leora's been killed! She was shot!"

Leora was very close to us. She and Mother had been best friends since middle school. She often came down from Dedham to stay with us at the shore, and after she married and moved to Pittsburgh, the visiting went on as before. Uncle Myron was part of it. The only regret about Myron was that he was a golfer and not a fisherman as we were in our family; but he was accommodating and could be jollied into wading in for smallmouth on a gray day.

Mother was choked and bewildered and kept saying in an unearthly groaning voice I had never heard before, "What do you mean? Leora? What do you mean? What do you mean? Leora?"

It seemed to me that she was angry with me, which was unreasonable. I had interrupted her kind of sewing that is done on a small linen drumhead. She thrust the tambourine, her fingers extended as if to take me by the shoulder to shake out the nonsense as she had when I was younger. I wasn't sure she would remember the needle. I flinched and looked to Dad.

When my father clenches his jaw, the muscles become bone, his lips bulge as if they have under them the pads a dentist slips in to take up saliva. He has never been a slack man in mind or body and does not appreciate it in others. He assessed the possibility of error in a twelve-year-old boy.

He held a finger up toward Mother to ask her to hold back and asked me to say again what I had heard. He went to the phone.

Instead of calling Uncle Myron as I expected, he asked for Pittsburgh information, and then the number of the police station nearest the Sherroder address.

The questions he asked the police desk and the way he hung up said enough. Separating the more-or-less-known from the said-to-be-known, the police were able to say that they had received a report by telephone at 9:47 P.M. from a man stating that he was the husband of the deceased. The witness at the scene stated that he had found Mrs Sherroder on the floor of the garage, apparently dead, apparently as a consequence of multiple wounds, apparently from shotgun fire. It had happened a little more than an hour ago and the investigation was just beginning. Dad made this report piece-meal in a halting voice while he held Mother.

"I'd better call Myron," he said, gently letting her go.

Myron hadn't realized it was already on the radio. The detectives were there taking pictures and asking questions, and he had been waiting for an opportunity to break away and make the call. After they spoke awhile Dad said, "Life is long, Myron. Take every day one at a time. I'll be there on an early plane," and hung up.

Mother had her voice under control. "What did he say?"

"He doesn't know much more than we do. Leora went to an evening meeting of the Handicapped Services board. He had the television on to a wildlife documentary and didn't hear a thing. When it was past the time Leora usually got home he walked out and saw the garage door open. She was lying beside the car. She was shot. They haven't found a gun."

While Mother made the family phone calls, Dad went to the window and stood fully ten minutes with his hands behind his back, staring through the dark at the few stars of houses on the far side of the bay. Mother left Grandma Dewaine for him. He could have waited until morning and seen Grandma on his way to the airport, but it would have been awful if she heard it first from a reporter calling to ask if she had a photo-graph of her daughter. He told her that Leora had died in an accident without suffering and that he would stop by in the morning. Being prepared in this way she could be relied on to get through the night. Dewaines managed. She was a Dewaine by assimilation.

Mother was also that much a Dewaine, but only that much. She took the phone and asked Grandma if she would like somebody to spend the night with her. She would be glad to come up herself. Would she like Dad to be with her. Would she like her good friend Betty Morse to be called. Mother listened to the timbre of Grandma saying No, that was unnecessary, she would be all right; and was satisfied. It was left as before that her son would stop there early on his way to the airport.

Although Dad had anyhow decided to take the Pittsburgh flight in order to be with Myron on the first difficult day, our family assumed that burial would be in the Dewaine plot in Brewster. When he called to give Myron his flight number, he learned that the service and burial would be in Pittsburgh.

"I don't understand such a decision," Mother said. "Leora has no family in Pittsburgh. They have been married so few years. Myron's family is out West. Your mother is only a two-hour ride from Brewster. It is inconsiderate to bury Leora in Pittsburgh. She ought to be in your family plot. Did you say that to him?"

"I made the case. It's Myron's decision to make. I can understand that he would want her nearby."

"There are others to think about."

"They have many friends in Pittsburgh."

"Friends are not family. Friends do not come to visit your grave site. It is a strange decision."

"It may be arbitrary but it isn't strange. It's his decision to make. It isn't easy to argue at a time like this."

"When is a good time? After the burial?" I seldom heard Mother that sharp with Dad.

"He and Leora chose the site with care. In his view, he is accommodating her wishes."

"In his view."

We all went to Pittsburgh for the funeral.

When people have lived their years it is possible to take satisfaction in memory, and even for levity to soften grief, and after long illness it is possible to speak of relief, but this was a day of harsh, unrelieved mourning, the most solemn day of my life. In the chapel, Uncle Myron sat between his brother Andrew and my father, and beside Father was Grandma Dewaine. Then Uncle Tom Dewaine, then Mother. They sat by bloodline. Except around a dinner table I had never before, at an occasion, seen Father not sit beside

Mother. Because of the nature of the wound the casket was closed.

Very little was said among us. When Grandma shook with hidden sobs, Dad took her hand. I did the same to my sister, at first awkwardly; then, when she clutched it to show how glad she was to have it, with (I suppose the right word is) pride.

After the cemetery Mother took Marnie and me directly to the plane. She did not want to stay over. She said tomorrow was a school day and we should be back. My father spent the rest of the day in Pittsburgh with Myron, talking to the police and the district attorney. They posted a reward.

2

You may have forgotten the story by now or may have it confused with the celebrated case of the Cleveland doctor's wife. The death of Leora Dewaine Sherroder was much less a story than the Cleveland story but it was closely followed in Pittsburgh and on Cape Cod where there are three columns of Dewaines in the phone book. You call a Dewaine to put on a roof, survey your land, pick up your rubbish, send you a nurse. To fish out of Rock Harbor, you sign on the *Cape Corsair*, Cap'n Pres Dewaine. You bank with Leo at Samoset 5¢ Savings. To cater a wedding you call Carolyn.

Dewaines hidden by marriage under other names must be many columns more. The only big rich Dewaines I know of are Ananders, through Cousin Peg. Delbert Anander knew what land to buy and how long to hold it, and how to run a bank and when to sell it. My father was the fourth Dewaine with the hardware and heating store, the first with the oil trucks.

The story in the newspaper about the will gave me an uncomfortable insight that others might not see Aunt Leora's death as I did. It didn't say anything that wasn't already known in the family: except for named bequests, everything was left to Uncle Myron as remainderman. They had no chil-

dren. Simply stating in the newspaper that Myron was Leora
Dewaine's heir seemed to imply something.

In follow-up stories, Leora became the heiress of the
Dewaine fortune, the Dewaines became Mayflower descen-
dants. The family had oil interests. A reporter discovered that
a brother of Leora's great-grandfather had been a governor
of Massachusetts; the family became politically influential.
Myron was a kidney specialist; he had been consulted by a
Mellon; he was a member of a country club; he became a
socialite doctor. They had no children. The socialite doctor
was the sole heir.

With such people, in such an environment, all things are
possible. You don't have to go beyond your own mind.

Uncle Myron was my friend who took me to the zoo; and to
the museum to see the dinosaurus xylophony stretching
down the hall ("From *zonnng* on his nose"—Myron had
impressive range—"to *tinnngggg*"); and to Three Rivers Sta-
dium to see a big-league baseball game.

We sat in a box behind first base. A high foul went up and I
saw that if it did not go up forever it would come down
sometime later that day right where I was. Everybody around
me stood up. I thought if I could get my hands on that ball I
could hold it.

The day was chilly, and the men wore gloves, but I was a
boy and of course hadn't thought I needed gloves. While my
head followed the nearly vertical rise of the ball Uncle Myron
grasped my left hand. "Here's a glove to take the sting out."
He raised his voice to the crowd around us. "Give the kid a
shot at it."

They cleared a space. I don't think any crowd today would
stand back to give a kid a shot. I followed the ball higher than
I had ever seen a ball go, while I worked the bunching out of
the palm of the glove and displayed the floppy fingers as a
target.

I was sure I was under it, but misjudged the angle of the
fall, backed into the men and finally fell backward into the
seats; and the ball, ignoring the chance to make a stylish

landing in a gray suede glove, dropped beyond my farthest
reach. My failure that day—despite the cooperation of the
entire world to help me succeed—is not yet forgotten. It
enhances the memory of Myron Sherroder, my friend, who
the newspaper said without saying it might have been the
one who killed Aunt Leora.

I began then to understand how words say things that
aren't in them. Words reach for meanings that are already
inside the hearer. In a card trick the magician fans out the
cards and says, "Pick one." Psych the cards as hard as you
want, you can't psych a ten of diamonds out of a tarot deck.
You have to take a card that's there. I wanted it another way,
but the statement that the husband of the murdered woman
was the beneficiary of her will picked up the card from my
standard human deck.

I began then to read about the case as others would. One
day at school I took a question from a friend—"How is your
uncle coming with that murder case?" It said to me that when
they spoke of Leora Sherroder's murder in their home, they
assumed that her husband, the socialite doctor who had
inherited her money, was probably complicit in some way.
And I could not help but think it too.

I was troubled. I didn't tell my father how I felt, but I put a
question in a form that betrayed me. "What if—?"

Before responding, my father laid his narrow eyes on me.
"That's the way people are. In this house we do not think like
that. My sister was a good judge of character. She chose your
Uncle Myron. As far as we know they had a good marriage."
Why "As far as we know . . .?"

I remembered too that when Dad called Myron that first
night he hadn't said to him that he thought he was innocent. I
wondered if Myron had noticed that.

I never heard my father say anything about innocence.
What I understood him to say was that we had to wait
respectfully, withholding judgment, as long as the process
took; forever, if necessary. We had a stake in the values of
organized society.

ustice

We were right to wait. In a few weeks the Pittsburgh police let it out that they were looking for a white man about forty years old with a butch haircut driving a late Plymouth white two door who had been seen several times in the neighborhood in the week of the murder and nobody knew who he was. They found what they believed was the gun in the Allegheny River about five miles from the house and began to trace it. The gun was a Winchester twelve. There are a lot of them around. We have one in our house.

That got the newspapers going again.

Dad went to Pittsburgh. He saw Uncle Myron. He talked to the district attorney and to Detective Gertner, who had the case from the beginning. Gertner said privately they weren't getting anywhere looking for the man in the Plymouth. There weren't any fingerprints on the gun; they hadn't been able to trace it.

The detective told Dad something else. He did not look at Mother as he reported it.

"They are talking to a woman they say Myron had been seeing before—" It's not easy to say *Before my sister was murdered.* "I have to say that bothers me."

"What did Myron say to that?" Mother asked.

"He's where he was. He knows they're looking into a lot of things."

"Did he say he knew what they were looking into?"

"He mentioned the gun and the man who had been seen in the neighborhood."

"That's all been in the papers. He didn't say anything about the woman?"

"He said 'and the usual gossip you can expect.'"

"Did he say what that was?"

"No, and I didn't ask him. He is a smart man. He can guess what comes to me."

It reinforced my impression that Myron was guilty. I was not so convinced that I would have been unable to be a fair juror; but I thought it probable, and I was sure I was not alone in our house to think it—not since Father's "as far as we know . . ."—not since Mother's refusal to stay in Pittsburgh after the funeral, and the clipped severity of her manner when Myron's name came up. I was in a conspiracy not to acknowledge that a guest had made a bad smell and there was no dog to look at.

3

Uncle Myron was indicted for first-degree homicide—I don't know why the language needs another word for murder.

"That must mean he's pretty guilty," I said.

Expressing judgment in an important matter made me feel important. I didn't know that before the law you are either guilty or not, there is no pretty to it.

My father stiffened his lips. "I don't want that said again in my hearing. A trial is to find that out. We have the adversarial system in this country as the best way to get at the truth. There is nothing like two sides putting up the best argument they know how. You may think you know Uncle Myron's defense, but you don't till you hear it argued. I don't want you to forget that."

Dad went to the trial to hear the woman for himself for the two days she was a witness. She testified that she had carried the gun from the garage when Uncle Myron told her to and had thrown it in the river. Uncle Myron's lawyer brought out that she was seeking revenge because Myron had started to see other women. He brought out that she was an alcoholic. She and a former boyfriend were involved in a larceny, and the district attorney had made a deal to let her off a perjury charge in exchange for her testimony in the Sherroder case. She could even have been the one who committed the murder. Myron's lawyer brought all that out.

"She didn't make a very good witness," my father said. "Myron's lawyer doesn't think she will be convincing to the jury."

But there wasn't any doubt that Myron had something

going with her—she knew too much about his life for it to be otherwise.

Myron said she only knew enough to make up the rest in order to get the reward. "I'm sorry all this comes out in this way that must seem sordid to you," he said. "I can't blame you for what you must think."

"Of course he can't blame you," Mother said. "What are you supposed to think? Leora was your sister. Did he still pretend he hadn't been going out with other women?"

"He said he had done what a lot of men do and he apologized for it. He said Leora would have understood why he saw other women had she known, even if she might not necessarily have condoned it."

"Not necessarily. I should think."

Myron had said, "I am not asking you to tell me what you now think about this. I only want you to hear me when I say I had nothing to do with it. I am entirely innocent."

"What *do* you think?" Mother asked.

My father's jaw muscles became bone. "I wasn't hired to be God," he said.

The afternoon the case went to the jury it was expected that deliberations probably wouldn't start until the next day. I was in bed with the lights out and the radio button in my ear when a bulletin came on that the jurors had decided to convene to test their sentiment. They found they had a verdict right away. The judge was coming in to hear it.

I got up and told Mother and Dad. We sat in the library and waited.

None of us made a guess what the verdict would be. It wasn't a ball game or somebody's else's family or anything that doesn't count and you can show how smart or how dumb you are. When something is close to you, you don't look at it the same way as if you're separated from it. In traffic the car ahead of you can be in the middle and won't get out of the way and you get mad. When you're in position to go around, you see it's somebody you know well and you cool off. You wave. Anything that is close to you is different.

The verdict was "Not Guilty."

To tell the truth, I didn't feel the relief you would expect from knowing that my uncle wouldn't have to spend the rest of his life in jail or be electrocuted. I certainly wouldn't have taken any joy from a guilty verdict, but it would have been more fitting and satisfying to human nature.

I suppose I am saying that my Aunt Leora, of my father's blood and therefore of mine, had been murdered, and that the way we are made requires that somebody be accountable. Almost any somebody rather than nobody. I'm the first to agree that for the sake of civilization we must respect the verdict of a court; still it isn't necessarily satisfactory to our natural sense of what is just.

I sensed that my mother felt the same, and for a moment that my father did too, but he said abruptly, "That's the verdict. The reward stands. We are going to look that much harder."

He called Uncle Myron and told him he knew the experience had been hard but he hoped he could get on with his life. He invited him to do some fishing. They arranged a weekend. Mother said, "You invited him *here*? I would just as soon you hadn't."

"I don't want to lose touch."

"I will never be comfortable with Myron. But it's up to you. I suppose men understand these things better." I supposed that wasn't what she thought.

4

Uncle Myron was grateful that we made him one of us. The truth is that without Leora he was a foreign substance. He could not attach himself by shaking my hand and telling me I grew an inch a week; by swinging my sister in the air; by trying to find a place to kiss on Mother's averted cheek. Dad hurried him through the greetings and got him to the stairs of the tower room overlooking the bay. He and Leora always had that room.

Next day was raw and drizzly, an ordinary April day. A good breeze came across from the northeast and the tide went out all morning. The open bay wouldn't be very comfortable. I thought they would fish Drum Pond, but Dad said, "Myron, have you ever fished Shelf Lake with me?" Uncle Myron couldn't remember that they had.

I don't think Myron ever fished before he married Leora. As often as not when they visited, he would go over and play Great Dune while the rest of us went to a bass pond. Dad certainly wasn't going to play golf and he didn't offer any choices.

"We'll go over there. We'll get some shelter from the wind. I have a new suit of Red Ball waders you can break in for me. I'll wear my old one."

They loaded rods, boots, waders, parkas, slickers, boxes of lures, leaders, spare lines and tools, and a lunch. They were ready for bass or trout all day in any weather. They dropped me at Everbloom Nursery where I had a Saturday-morning job.

Bob Everbloom and I were moving azaleas from the back field to front beds, beginning in a drizzle we knew would get heavier, and when it did Bob decided we had enough of outside work. I could have worked under glass but I didn't come to do that. I liked to be outside on weekends. I said I would skip it, they didn't need me in the greenhouse. I borrowed Bob's bike and headed for Shelf Lake. They were carrying enough extra tackle to outfit me.

All this country around here, all of Cape Cod, is the tailings left after the great glacier thawed and backed off to Canada. It's all rock brought down by the ice and melted out, pockets of sandy soil from old oceans washing over, and a skin of topsoil from decay. Those big stands of trees are in sand not too far down, then rock. The only clay is wherever you happen to dig your foundation; you can't get drainage, I never saw it fail.

After the margin sand Shelf Lake is a basin of underwater boulders and tables of rock fed by springs and the runoff from Spark's Hill. The surrounding land is in conservation. What falls they let lie. The bones of old downed trees lie around the rim. Those spines of big fish stuck in the ground are dead cedars. A couple of paths lead in through heavy woods.

It was too raw a day for people to come for wilderness walks, and most of the fishermen around here are either commercial and need the quantities they get in saltwater or they want the fast action of bay fishing. Our Jeep was the only vehicle parked at NO VEHICLES PERMITTED BEYOND THIS SIGN. On a busy day there might be two. I locked the bike to the Jeep's bumper and went down the woods path.

Nearing the bottom I heard my father call, "Left, farther left, toward the cove."

Through the trees I glimpsed that they were both in hip-deep, Uncle Myron a hundred or so yards west and working farther. Rain dimpled the water. Away from the lea of the hill, fans of wind patterned the surface like shoaling fish. I was troubled by something but didn't concentrate my attention on what it might be as I was busy picking through catbrier that snatched into the path.

"Another ten yards. They're in there," my father called out.

Then I realized what troubled me. Myron was on the edge of the shelf that gave the lake its name. It fell off without any warning into a deep hole. I took a running step and opened my mouth to shout but it hardly got out when he let out a bellow and pitched down.

My mind churned with what could be done and what I had to do. I could get around to the shoreline nearer to him, and dive in and help him out of his gear. I could—

But I didn't move because more dumbfounding to me than the accident itself was that my father acted as though it wasn't happening. He heard Myron and saw him flail to stay afloat and go under in seconds. He knew as I did that Myron, under the roiled water, fought to get out of his parka and sweater, then out of the waders that were filling and turning into anchors; and my father turned away and cast. I was locked on dead center. Dad began to reel in. His rod bent. He had a bass fighting and flopping like a sand-filled stocking. Working light tackle, he had to give and take carefully not to lose it. The ripples settled out of the water where Myron had been — it was erased! — and my father was unslipping the net with his free hand and playing the bass with the other.

I was terrified — not frightened, terrified — as much for my father as for myself. He had deliberately led my uncle to be drowned. I tried to make it happen differently in my mind, but I could not doubt what I had seen and heard.

When at last I found the will to move, it was not toward him but back up the trail, to be away and alone long enough to get my bearings before I had to face him.

I rode the bike in the rain to the nursery and put it in the toolshed. Nobody was around. I didn't have to talk to anybody.

Behind the mall down the road from Everbloom's the receiving platforms stood on iron legs, backed against the cement block, the cheap side of the stores. Weather swept over the blacktop, pooling where the graders hadn't got it right. On raw bulldozed ground beyond the blacktop, weeds and a few stringy locusts tried to start a forest again. A tree line the bulldozers wouldn't get to for a few years failed into the mist at the end of this world. Nobody ever came back there unless a truck was unloading. I hunched under a dock.

As the evidence against Uncle Myron had become stronger and weaker and stronger again in the year that had passed since Aunt Leora's death, I had felt in myself many times the sufficient certainty that he had killed her so that I could imagine myself doing to him as my father had.

I had imagined aiming the gun — the same gun, the twelve-gauge, to make the justice more shapely — and firing. I could do that, I had told myself.

Under the shelter of the platform, I knew I had only been telling myself a story. I could have put my finger on the trigger but not pulled. I might have led him to step off the shelf, but duty as I understood it, as I had learned it from my father, would have compelled me to save a drowning man even if I had been the one who put him in peril.

I had had the chance and not used it. I had not burst out of the trees shouting. I had not waded in. I had watched; then run to get the bike.

My father had pulled the trigger and turned away as if it were nothing.

I drowned in questions. Why had I done nothing? Was it because I was young and not much was expected of me? Was it because it had happened in the presence of my father, and it was not my place to put myself forward where he did not? Was I bound to silence forever? What would happen if he were suspected? And stories were in the paper?

And he went on trial?

Would I come forward to witness for him to say that his account of the event was whatever he said it was? Would I be able to stick with a lie like that—for my father, who had made lying a hard thing for me to do?

What if somebody in one of the cars that had passed on the road recognized me? What if it was reported and I was taken to the police station and asked what I knew and why I had not volunteered it before?

What was expected of me? I had nobody to ask.

The rain drew off. I would have to go home. I took with me the simplest of stories to account for myself. I had biked to Nickerson Park, in the direction of Shelf Lake, and when the rain began had got under the cover of a firewood shed.

A diver found Uncle Myron bundled at the foot of the shelf in forty feet of water. It was never discussed after my father explained that Myron had been warned, that he must have lost track of where he was while my father had been inattentive. Anybody who knew that water and how you could become engrossed working a five-pound bass on a three-pound line understood how easily it happened.

Myron's brother came to the Cape to make arrangements to ship the body to Pittsburgh for burial alongside Aunt Leora. He was Uncle Andrew to me, although we never knew that family very well. They were westerners, we were easterners, we met only at anniversary parties, weddings, funerals.

He said Myron had been a good brother and he would miss him. I suppose in some way he felt that my father had a degree of responsibility as the accident had happened in our territory, so to speak, but he didn't indicate it.

The circumstances were such that the card of suspicion never turned over in anybody's head. Nobody who knew Ben Dewaine would have thought it for an instant.

5

I lived difficult years with my father after that, although all the difficulties were within me. On the surface our close relationship was undisturbed. We fished and hunted together as before, and I took many problems to him for a viewpoint.

As I had declared against going into the family business it was thought that I might become a lawyer. I have an orderly mind and some ability to express myself and therefore thought it too. I was well along in college before I decided to do other work. In those early years, the years in which we allow ourselves to think abstractly, I often reflected about justice, but I never allowed myself to discuss it with my father, fearing that one word would take me to another until I reached one that I would regret.

I came to have considerable respect for Pilate. I thought how much more difficult Pilate's problem may have been than the press reported. I would want to know more about what kind of man Pilate was before I concluded that he had a worn-out conscience or that he had settled for an epigram.

Nine years later the man with the brush haircut turned himself in.

He couldn't live with it. It happens all the time. They see the victim's face at night and think of what a life is and what it is to destroy one, and they get disgusted with themselves. They begin to think there may be Eternal Judgment after all and they will be accountable. They show up at police stations and have to convince desk officers that they aren't nuts. They call up reporters and meet them in diners. They ask priests to be go-betweens. They hire lawyers to get them the best deal.

The man's name was Rome Hurdicke.

Again it was a story in the papers. He had parked, looking for opportunity as he had on other nights, and this night a dark place beside the lane beyond the Sherroder house had been the cover that attracted him. He had followed Aunt Leora into the garage intending to bluff her with the gun. She had been slow to respond. He thought she was about to call for help. He panicked and shot her and then thought only about getting away. The most singular event in two lives, and it was from beginning to end so ordinary that it could have been set in type like a slogan to be called up with a keystroke.

The newspapers rehashed it and added the strange fate that befell so many people associated with the crime. Four of the jurors were dead. The judge had been killed in a private plane accident. The woman who claimed to be the well-known socialite doctor's mistress committed suicide. The husband of the murdered heiress drowned in a fishing accident on Cape Cod.

There could be no doubt Hurdicke was the man. He told them where and when he had bought the gun, and they verified the numbers. They found the Plymouth still in service, three owners forward and a coat of white paint two coats down. It was an old case, and as he had turned himself in he got twenty years and was eligible for parole in twelve.

And so, Uncle Myron's life had been taken without cause.

I think somebody—perhaps his brother Andrew—may care for Myron as we cared for Aunt Leora, and if he knew the circumstances of his death would yearn for human justice as my father did. I don't know. I can't deal with how Uncle

Andrew might feel. My father is my flesh and blood and he is a good man.

I can't deal with my own guilt. If I had responded on the instant that I saw Uncle Myron pitch into the water could I have saved him?

I don't know. I will never get over not making the attempt, but confession offers me no way out, for it would be to witness against my father. I am tribal enough to say that my duty is to him, to keep the secret. In some matters it is true that what is not known does not exist. It exists for us who know it.

After Hurdicke confessed I watched my father closely. I trembled that he might turn himself in or even take his own life in remorse. I didn't know if he would be more likely to do it if he knew that I knew his secret, or if he thought he alone knew what had happened at Shelf Lake. As a son who had become also a father I knew that some fragment of his life he intended to be an object lesson for me, but I couldn't know how much.

His manner, naturally reserved, became wintry. He gave up his places on church and hospital boards, and reduced his responsibilities at the company. Time passing without incident did not lull me to suppose that he had made his peace with Uncle Myron's ghost, any more than Hurdicke had made his with Aunt Leora's. Nevertheless, he went on with his life in a normal way, at a lowered tone, into his retirement years.

He entered then a remission in which he seems to have regained his appetite for a more active life. Mother said the other day, "He had a new garden turned over. He is talking about going west in the fall to hunt ram. He rejoined his skeet club. I think he is coming into good years."

That may be, but I have marked my calendar.

I don't know how Father accepts that the sentence of the man who killed his sister has been commuted to time served. Hurdicke will be released next week. I can hope only that my father has had enough of dealing out justice on earth.

"It Is Hard for Thee to Kick—"

1

SHE read the weekly *Cape Cod Fog* to keep up with who died and who was exhibiting where. She scanned the letters page to see if anybody she knew had written. She closed her mind to the chatter from the TV.

Amelia didn't know what Leland expected to learn from somebody who didn't have enough sense to put on his hat in the rain. This wasn't even rain, it was sleet—the news talker *said* it was sleet—and he stood there in the middle of it interviewing a man she recognized as a senator or a cabinet member and neither one had enough sense to put on a hat. No journalist and nobody in government since Franklin D. Roosevelt had enough sense to put on a hat in the rain. She had raised children who had more sense than that.

What Amelia liked best about TV were shredded pictures. She also liked the scramble patterns of cable stations. She painted with the Bay Painters and had an eye for pattern and color.

They sat in their wing chairs, having after-dinner coffee, in a room gathered from the decorating ideas of people who had lived two hundred years ago. Concessions to modernity went no further than wired lamps, Boehm porcelain birds nested on the shelves, and a Lladro figure (she thought it slinky, tacky, a spineless caricature of El Greco, but it had been a gift from her daughter-in-law). On the brass-galleried table between them a glistening crystal rock and a Chinese lamp with a boisterous street scene recalled vacations in the South-west and the Orient. The portraits and landscapes of Cape Cod on the walls were by her associates whose work she respected. Her own studies of changing seasons on the marsh were painted in a somewhat pointillist mode; they encouraged speculation that the artist might have more than the knack of rendering. Photos of children and grandchildren testified to a well-ordered life standing on the divide of its fiftieth year.

She went on to the editorial page and was arrested by a headline. She entered a state of mind in which she seldom found herself: she was mad.

"Leland, did you see what the *Fog* says about Marilyn Kauffmann on the water-rights thing?"

He allowed her one ear. "I haven't read the *Fog*."

"It says Marilyn is opinionated, self-centered, destructive and petulant."

"She is sure wrong on the water rights. Leave it up to that crowd and every acre of land in town will be a park. She won't get any votes on this." He had the leading real-estate agency in town and knew about those things.

"They can disagree with Marilyn without slamming her. She wouldn't swat a fly."

"Only damn fools pay any attention to what's in a newspaper."

He had kept quiet about it, but he wasn't as keen as the women and the conservation crowd were about those mosquito-breeding swamps. Marilyn Kauffmann always had her name in the paper saving some marsh or other or going at the Planning Board about water tables. That was all well and good, nobody was in favor of polluting anything, but those people overdid. It was kind of a racket with them. Not that they weren't good people, but they never had to earn a living in their own business, never paid any attention to the tax rate, just kept on buying marshes and tying up builders with questions to the Planning Board. Marilyn Kauffmann was so far out on this water-rights thing that even her own crowd said so.

"If nobody pays attention, what do we buy them for?"

He didn't mean nobody paid attention. He meant that the newspaper was for the stock tables, the scores, the real-estate ads, the drift of things, not every last word. "She doesn't have to worry. People who know her walk by that stuff."

"Everybody doesn't know her. They know what Mel Brate tells them."

He retired from the conversation. He thought Brate was the smartest man around. Came to town thirty years ago, started up a paper in a nothing little Cape Cod town, and now pissed money in the hottest real-estate market in the U.S.A. Made more money from real-estate ads than all the real-estate offices in town made from selling the property itself, and on top of it got the award for editorials on conservation. How could you fault that?

At the post office next morning Amelia glimpsed, as she stamped in out of the sleet that had arrived from Washington, one of those public-spirited people manning a clipboard with a petition and wearing the sheepish face of a man discovered doing work beneath his station.

The petition monger picked up the glimpse and locked on. He knew the woman—Lee Roulter's wife? Haseley's wife?—who paused to obey the sign requesting that she PLEASE WIPE SHOES ON MAT. He was beginning to feel lonely. He hadn't realized he knew so few people in town outside the Abimelech Lane Association, and they all acted as if they were doing him a big favor instead of the other way around. They didn't appreciate the importance of what he was doing. They didn't understand that he never signed petitions either if he could avoid it, and he couldn't remember the last time he went to a town meeting, but this was different. This didn't affect only Abimelech Lane, this affected property rights all over town.

He kept after his memory to give him a connection and found her wearing this same green trench coat and glossy rain hat, standing in a movie line with Lee Roulter. The Roul-

ters lived in West Bay, the next private way down from Abimelech. He ought to be able to get her to sign.

"Good morning, Mrs Roulter. Come in out of the rain."

"Hello there. Better in here than out there." Who was he?
She was standing still for his pitch. A live one.

"Jack Fasten here."

"Of course," she said. Della Fasten's. "How's Della?"

"We're all fine. Got past a little flu. I see you're keeping Lee
healthy." He presented his clipboard. "This is to bring a
motion to the next town meeting to amend the Town Landing
Access Article. There's a sleeper in there they don't tell you
about. Do you realize that if Article 39 goes through without
amendment anybody who wants to can drive over any private road in town, not only Abimelech Lane? Your roads too.
You pay to keep up your road and any Tom, Dick and Harry
can use it as if he owned it. Can you imagine that the selectman have as little regard for private property as that? This is
the first time I ever asked anybody to sign a petition."

He wanted her to understand he wasn't one of those publicity hounds who wrote letters to the editor. He didn't call on
people to raise money even for his church, and until last
week it hadn't entered his head that he would push a petition
on anybody. Some people liked to do those things and there
seemed to be enough of them to go around.

And here he was, one of them, driven by a half-hour in the
cold to take the shelter of the lobby, running his book beside a
barrel where people were throwing the second catalogs, the
third-through-twelfth free credit cards, anything labeled
IMPORTANT or CONFIDENTIAL or that looked like a fake
telegram or a solicitation from the other party or a flier about
lumber sales, investments, mistreated Indians or starving
children in still another one of those damn places. Stuff. Stuff
was wedged so tight in their boxes they could hardly get a
grip on it to haul it out, and after they finished tossing and
keeping three letters and a magazine and a soap sample, they
didn't want to get involved with petitions. Mrs. Roulter, however, was accommodating —

"Do I get your signature? I never before carried a petition for a thing."

While he had been rambling on about a matter she was aware had some importance but she knew would be sorted out by others, not herself, she had been looking at his face as closely as manners permitted. She was blessed with land-scape everywhere, out of every window, on every walk. She would never have enough time to paint the changing colors on the meadows and marshes, the old houses and skeletons of boats that sat for her as long as she had the patience for them. But she had begun to draw faces in her sketchbook, and last week had put one up on her easel.

She couldn't use Fasten's face, she couldn't see any *reason* to paint it. She wasn't good at faces and needed bones to hang a portrait on—the kind of armature any Cape Cod marsh or falling-down shingle house gave her. Most faces looked like bars of soap that had been carved and then used by the family for a week.

"All right."

Unaware that he had no eyes, no nose, no jaw, no usable hairline, Fasten thought he was doing pretty good to hold Roulter's wife to hear about his binge of public service. She had finished signing and writing her name and address, and he still had her.

She thought she had done her duty and inclined away politely.

He inclined with her. Maybe he had bagged the ultimate prize—she might stand someplace else and get others to sign. He had asked Carla Meyers, his nextdoor neighbor, if she would get signatures at the bank, but she said she never did things like that, as though it were high-tech sex.

He said to Amelia, "It's easy to get signatures once people understand what it is."

Amelia sensed that she was about to be asked to take a petition around West Bay. She thought she had given away enough of her life to Jack Fasten.

"Good luck," she said. "I have to get home."

The encounter reminded her that she ought to do something to support Marilyn Kauffmann. She might write a letter to the paper to let people know what kind of person Marilyn really was, how much she had done for the town. Thirty eight hundred people knew what was in the *Fog*, but only a handful knew Marilyn.

Amelia had once written to the paper to praise the Rescue Squad for its efficient response when her father had the heart attack. She had been one of twelve signers of a letter endorsing a request to the town to provide a budget for plantings in front of the Highway Department toolshed. But to sit down and inscribe on her Canada Goose notepaper a reproof to the editor of the paper because of something he wrote about Marilyn Kauffmann—she just didn't know how to get the right tone for that. She had to think what effect it would have on Leland's business to have her in public like that. She didn't think she would like to be seen as someone who volunteered to enter a controversy.

She settled on telephoning Marilyn. She didn't know her in a truly personal way, had been in her house only once, but considered her a friend.

"Amelia, how nice to hear you." An old woman's voice; fine, strained through silk.

"I just wanted to tell you how badly I feel about what *The Fog* said. I thought it was uncalled for."

"How nice of you to say so. That's Melvin Brate. One can't be surprised."

"You're generous. I'm sure a lot of people will tell you they feel as I do."

"That's very thoughtful of you. We don't have much chance to win but we will have to do our best. Do you happen to know how Dr Scacz feels about the article?"

Marilyn misunderstood that the call was to support her on the water rights. "No, I haven't talked to anybody."

"It would be very nice if you would ask him, if you felt you could. I have so much calling to do and I don't have much voice left."

A moment's pause to untangle her tongue. "I could do that. His walk-around sometimes crosses mine. If I miss him on the road I'll call him."

"If you would do that and let me know I would be ever so grateful."

Amelia made a point to be on the lane at four-thirty on a lowering wintry afternoon to intercept Scacz—earmuffed and Red Sox sweatshirted—coming along in the dusk at his usual rate that implied a purpose to get it over with and be back in his study for the one scotch allowed before dinner. Scacz was emeritus in political science at Harvard, an advisor to presidents and governors, his subject Public Opinion. He knew what was known and what was not known, although he seemed not to know anything about the present moment as he booted toward her, ignoring potholes and ice-greased ruts, elbows high and flailing righteously, attention tilted upwards like that of a man trying to catch sight of his own eyes. It would be slowing down a train to get more than his standard quick grin.

She semaphored an arm.

"Hello there, girl," he said, offsetting an earmuff enough to be available. An extremely busy man whose time one ought to be considerate of. He stressed his ankles to maintain a semblance of exercise. She had an after-vision of his legs still pumping. He wouldn't know her name, which was the reason she hadn't telephoned.

"Doctor Scacz, I don't want to interrupt your walk. Marilyn Kauffmann asked me, if I happened to run into you, to ask how you stood on the Water Rights Article."

"I haven't the faintest, girl." He had no more to say.

"Thank you. That's an answer. I'll tell her."

"It hasn't a chance of prevailing so it isn't worth thinking about."

"You've thought that much about it. I'll tell her."

"The selectmen are against it. The Finance Committee is against it. The Reform Committee is against it. The business community is against it. The letters are all on the other side, except Marilyn's. Isn't your husband in real estate? He's against it. What is on that girl's mind to think she can get two-thirds?''

She was pleased that Scacz knew her specifically, not only as a neighborhood face. It was the first she had heard about two-thirds. She had thought if you got the most votes you won. It was America.

"Two-thirds?"

"Of course, girl. It's a two-thirds issue, it amends zoning. Not a chance. Does Marilyn have any troops? She won't get anywhere without door-knockers and phone-callers. That's what issues are all about. I don't think the troops are out there on this. You can tell her I don't know why she wants to waste her time. She isn't that young anymore. How is Marilyn?"

"I haven't seen her for a month. I talked to her on the phone. She sounded usual."

"Good for her."

"I called to tell her I thought *The Fog* had been rude to her. I don't know whether you saw it."

"Yes," he said reflectively. "Scripture tells us 'It is hard for thee to kick against the pricks.'" Enjoying his sally, he displayed teeth larger and squarer than she had supposed; Chiclets. Caved eyes. He would be relatively easy to sketch (*but was a cartoon art?*). If she could steel herself to look at him steadily and intrusively—impolitely—as if he were a marsh, she might ask him to sit while she searched his face for structure and light.

"Give the girl my blessing and tell her to save her strength." He positioned his earmuff and pumped off, elbowing aside the heavy winter air.

2

Amelia did not take away from her conversation with Marilyn Kauffmann, and the one that followed when she reported her conversation with Dr Scacz, the impression that Marilyn's friends with whom she had been through so many years—to grass the dunes, to stop them from filling marshes with road rubble and dumping oil in the woods and septage in the ponds—had rallied to her, had even telephoned.

It seemed so—out of proportion—that Marilyn should be alone in her cottage while Melvin Brate, surrounded by respectful employees and supplicants for his favor, scolded her for being something she was not and issued thick Special Sections advertising half-million and million-dollar houses (Leland had just listed the Bahner house for *two-and-a-half million—in West Bay!*) to be lived in by people who didn't give a hoot that tonight Marilyn would be in a committee meeting, tomorrow she would get hold of a legislator and go to a hearing in Boston, and every day write a letter to two and call a few people so that forty years from now a glass of drinkable water might still be had on Cape Cod.

That everybody said she was wrong on this water-rights thing didn't license Mel Brate to jeer at her. Compensation of some kind seemed to be owed Marilyn.

Amelia considered what she herself would appreciate in the circumstances, and it seemed little enough. She would want to get the kind of telephone call she had just made to Marilyn. Nothing more than that. But it should come from somebody who meant a great deal to Marilyn. If Laura Jane Driskle, the Red Queen, called—

Amelia had her index open to the *D*'s, the phone off the cradle and her finger on the dial, and drew back. It was not her style to intrude. She had fulfilled the mission Marilyn gave her. On the scale of human virtue it was more or less sufficient in what was not really her affair. She replaced the phone in the cradle and closed the index. She was too much drawn away from her studio these days.

As the week passed and the night of the meeting approached, Amelia realized that Wednesday was their season-ticket night at The Cinema. They had a picture by an Indian director whose name she forgot but whose work she admired. She hoped Leland would feel he could miss this special town meeting, it wasn't as important as the annual. The agenda published in the *Fog* was a new cruiser for the police, hiring two part-time firemen, Fasten's Town Landing Access article about which she hadn't seen or heard a word anywhere except that day in the post office, Marilyn Kauffmann's article, transferring funds from account A to account B, paving this, taking that. She mentally added the unpublished agenda: Does anybody wish to be heard on the motion, and some bearded old crank accepting the offer, and all that Stuff?

Marilyn's article was a reason to stay away. Amelia Roulter would only be one more vote against; even the League had come out against.

The night before the meeting a storm came down from Alberta, and the Boston TV reporter and the mayor stood hatless in the weather. Frost grew in their hair as in a speeded-up film on aging. By morning Alberta weather had deposited a treasure of snow on Cape Cod, if you weren't a highway commissioner who had to figure how to get rid of it, and gone to sea.

From the breakfast-room window, the panorama from their yard around to the river and the marsh lay unmarked except for cowflops off the ends of branches, and Leland's boot tracks to the turn of the driveway for the morning paper. Small birds stood in the bushes waiting for bluejays to clear the feeder. Junipers, like hampered eagles, struggled to lift their wings from the weight of drift. Thaw already dripped from the roof. June might have perfect days, but January had some too. The Florida crowd was missing this.

Leland's head was down on his sports page. It seemed to her an inadequate occupation for such a morning. She wished he would be as struck as she was by the fragile island of ice floating down the river, honeycombed with air like a raspberry ice ball they used to sell for a dime, dissolving; it would be gone unseen except for this moment.

"I'd like to see that movie tonight," she said.

"You go ahead. I saw one of those Indian movies last year. I'm not going to the meeting. They don't need me. I may watch the Celtics."

In thirty years of marriage she hadn't entered a theater without Leland, except to take the children to a matinee. Why it was necessary to be accompanied in order to sit in silence was not to be explained. It was part of her life, the way things were done. To be free to go alone gave her a problem.

By afternoon she decided she didn't feel like driving all the way to Dennis on roads that would freeze slick again after dark to sit alone at a movie. When Leland arrived from the office she told him she was going to the town meeting.

He said, "Watch out, there's still ice on the back road. You're sure you don't want to catch the Celtics?"

"No, I already told Marilyn I'd pick her up."

"You're not going to get involved in that, are you?"

"I just thought she would rather not drive."

3

It was a bigger meeting than it would have been if Jack Fasten hadn't had the letter in the paper and talked it up on Abimelech Lane and at the post office. As many as seventeen voters who might not otherwise have shown up were there on his alert. When Amelia and Marilyn signed in and got their voting cards the moderator already had his quorum and was calling up the first article.

The Middle School gym was a cement block room with bleacher benches on the long walls and camp chairs lined up on the basketball court. Marilyn knew where she wanted to sit to be able to get at the microphone. She took off across the front of the room, between the voters and the town officials seated behind the row of end-to-end knockdown banquet tables. Keeping up, Amelia felt alarmingly prominent. Customarily the Roulters turned toward the rear after getting their voting cards, then came forward on one of the aisles to a somewhat midway location.

The meeting droned on with Stuff after Stuff they ought to be able to take care of without reading eternally long paragraphs in legalese. Conferences she didn't understand took place between the town counsel and the moderator and between the selectmen and among the finance-committee members. She had been to a Greek Orthodox service with all that mysterious activity going on behind screens. Town meetings seemed to her a less colorful Greek service.

The sound equipment was not the best; it emitted a haze of collateral reverberation, lost the softer-spoken speakers, squealed like a mothering animal if approached too close. She read into the packet of literature she had taken from the registration table — texts of articles to be acted on, pamphlets advocating or objecting.

Eventually they got to the first business that interested her, Article 39, the Town Landing Access Article that upset Fasten. She read it over while they debated the previous article, whether something or other should be done with an old generator. She saw what Fasten was talking about but wasn't altogether persuaded that anybody like him could see something everybody else overlooked. Leland agreed with Fasten, though, so there was something to it. She was ready to honor her signature on his petition and support him. If the selectmen and the Finance Committee stood their ground, though, she would have to see how others felt.

A selectman offered the Town Landing Access Article, droning on clause after clause that (like poetry) couldn't be understood through the ear, and (unlike poetry) made no satisfactory, if senseless, noise such as Kranitz made when he read at the library last month. If they hired Kranitz to read the articles, people would get a better idea if they liked them or not.

"There is an oversight in the article as printed," the selectman said, raising his head for attention. "As written it may be construed to allow access over private ways. Insert on the fifth line after the word ways, *semi-colon except nothing in this article as written shall be construed to allow such traffic over private ways period.*"

"Is there a second?" the moderator inquired. He heard it from an unidentifiable source. "Does anybody wish to be heard?"

While Jack Fasten—deprived of the Call to Arms speech he had been reworking for two weeks, his amendment now a useless piece of paper—was making up his mind whether he wished to be heard to thank the selectmen for curing the defect, the moderator asked if they were ready for the question.

The house was unanimous except for three voices that thought they were still voting on what to do with the generator. Fasten didn't know whether his petition had raised the subject (as his friends assured him) or whether he could have accomplished the same purpose by getting hold of a selectman on the phone; or whether the selectmen, as they said, had themselves seen the error too late to correct the printed sheet and had done the next best thing. He left after the vote as the business he had come for was concluded, the people who liked to go to meetings could handle the Stuff, and like any sane man he wanted to see as much of the Celtics game as remained.

"I want to tell you," Amelia said as Marilyn gathered her papers, prepared to move her article when the moderator called her, "I may not vote with you. I won't vote against you—" Marilyn looked at her with a gentle smile "—I may not vote at all."

"Of course, dear. Vote as you wish."

Not a large woman but sturdy, Marilyn stalked toward the microphone, lay her papers on the podium, and explained in her silken voice—not easy to hear, it would require others to take up the details and argue them clearly for her, and Scacz had said she had no troops—why the town needed the option to buy water rights it was not now able to pay for.

The moderator asked for a second. When none was immediately apparent, Amelia steeled herself to make a slight supportive noise—had already cleared her throat, seconding was not voting—but it was unnecessary as the moderator discovered his second again in the supply he kept hidden in the audience.

Did any one wish to be heard?

Yes, many did. The chairman of the Finance Committee wished to say on behalf of a unanimous committee what an awful idea this was. The president of the Board of Trade and the president of the Taxpayers Association argued the same. Marilyn Kauffmann had the worst idea since New York clam chowder.

Others spoke from here and there in the house, adding information about tax rates, the Commonwealth Statutes, what had happened upstate in a similar matter an impressive amount of knowledge was lodged in that civilian body. At least one speaker was on Marilyn's side; and possibly two more, Amelia couldn't be sure which side they were arguing, but they seemed supportive.

As the mover, Marilyn held her ground at the podium, standing aside and listening attentively as others came to the microphone or spoke from one of the microphones traveled around the floor by pages from the High School Civics Club. She spoke once again, offering figures to refute something Amelia hadn't quite heard.

Amelia felt they were all missing the point anyhow, they were talking about *Issues, Issues, Issues*. The important thing was that Marilyn Kauffmann, a *person, a human being*, had been wounded. Hadn't anyone anything to say about that? Doris Gumpert, chairman of the League? Addie Anderson from the Water Board? The Red Queen? They were all there, they knew—

The moderator now warned the house that there was a great deal of business yet to accomplish, and speakers should limit themselves to as short a time as possible—a minute— and please not go over ground other speakers had covered, and—yes, the gentleman over there? who came forward, full of righteous wrath and smote Marilyn with the adjectives he had read in the newspaper—*opinionated, destructive, petulant!* and added from his own store of knowledge *a brash, thoughtless intrusion on the Planning Board's function*—. Amelia felt old-fashioned. She wanted to take a cane to him.

Uprose the Red Queen Laura Jane Driskle, chair of the Reform League, past-president of the League of Women Voters and the Garden Club and the Civic Association, trustee of the library and first female warden of the church, Marilyn's ally in a dozen good works. She approached the microphone with the deliberate majesty of a royal barge, soft Art Deco waves streaming beside each ear, a strawberry scarf her ensign.

Amelia felt a rush of elation. A battle would at last be joined. Those people and their *Issues*—

With practiced composure Laura Jane ticked a fingernail on the microphone to be sure it was on, unscrewed the device that held it four inches too low on its chrome stem, elevated it, ticked it again, paused, and spoke.

"We have in place a program that may not be perfect but is adequate until the voters have had a chance to study it. The issue is whether we should act precipitously—" *No, Laura Jane, no! The issue is whether Marilyn Kauffmann should be spoken of this way in the newspaper without* "or pass the problem to the Board of Health and the Planning Board for vetting. By law, the Boards are obliged to hold public hearings" —*anybody standing up and saying something*—

The Red Queen finished the debate with another decisive sentence (it was her style to sum up) and moved from the microphone to accustomed applause. The sense of the meeting was that everything that need be said had been said. No other hands were in the air to catch the moderator's survey.

With enough fear and loathing to last a lifetime, Amelia saw that it came down to her.

Never before had anything like this come down to her. Such matters were always taken care of without her involvement. To be exposed in such a singular position was alien to her desire and nature.

She filled her lungs and raised a hand for attention, modestly, not at full thrust; to be heard, not sure of what she would say, but to be heard.

She sensed around her restlessness that the matter was going on too long. Somebody mumbled "Call the question," which seemed like a good idea to others who also mumbled it. The moderator's eye came around with a *going going gone* look, caught Amelia's arm half raised, and pointed, "Yes? The lady?"

She got to her feet in confusion, trying to remember not only what she wanted to say but what it was necessary to do before she could say it. She must get to the aisle, walk to the microphone—*Call the question*—be sure the button was on—*Call the question*—speak clearly, close but not too close or there would be—*the question, Mr Moderator*—that awful squeal—

"Is the lady moving to call the question?"

"Yes," she said, meaning no, yes she wanted to be heard.

"We have a motion to call the question." The moderator's eyes left her. Seconds came from all around the house, while Amelia hung in bewilderment and Marilyn left the podium and came to resume her seat for the voting.

"I meant to speak," Amelia said in apology, reaching for Marilyn's hand as they again took their seats.

Marilyn could have said *Why didn't you then?* but she understood that some things that were her style were not the style of others.

"I appreciate very much all that you have done. You have been very considerate."

When the moderator asked for the ayes on the question, *Shall the Water Rights Article, Article 40, be approved?* Amelia was up promptly with Marilyn. She had failed Marilyn once and would not again. The scattering of voters on their feet testified to a lost cause—no more than a tenth of the house was with them. Knowing her own soul in ordinary times, Amelia guessed that a few others who might have been inclined to rise stayed seated to avoid notoriety.

Standing among so few, she could see all the seated—Laura Jane and Ted, Melvin Brate, Allie, Doris, the Elligotts, the Marises, all their friends. She found Scacz getting to his feet when the count had already begun. His wife, whatever her name was, followed. Amelia thought maybe she had accounted for two votes.

Her back got straighter as she stood, holding forward her voting card as the faithful interposed holy medals between themselves and evil spirits. After the teller clicked her into his counter, after Marilyn was down, Amelia Roulter was still up, looking around. She caught Scacz's eye. He gave a slight flick of a hand to acknowledge her and sat.

Standing there alone was the most liberating moment she could remember, all the way back to getting on the train for Wellesley. The swarm of negative votes that rose at the moderator's invitation did not bother her at all. She stood until Marilyn Kauffmann tugged her down so she would not be recorded on both sides of the question.

Lion Wagon

THE bus came over the crest and turned on yellow flashers. The slave lights pulsed over the driver's head, letting the kids whose stop it was know to get ready. Emory could hear them getting up in the back. They were going to crowd in the aisle. They were supposed to wait till it stopped. Emory didn't like it when somebody was between him and the window on one side and guys hung over his shoulder in the aisle on the other. It made him feel they had the power to shut off his air.

It wasn't only the crowding—they would block him from getting up when Dode did. He wouldn't be able to stand behind her and catch the smell that trailed from her open collar; he would risk for that.

He saw that it was only Rawl. He would have stayed back for Dex, but he could face Rawl. While the bus slowed at the sandpit he slid out of his seat and got ahead.

"Let's go," Rawl said to move him. Emory poked away the few seconds while Dode looked up to see if whoever was in the aisle was going to wait. She had brilliant eyes like his sister's doll that closed when it was put down, and opened when it was taken up. Her doll eyes asked him directly if he was going to let her have her turn. Licking at a frayed corner of lipstick was part of question. He let her in ahead to show that he was a gentleman. The guys said she put out, and if she had her choice of guys to put out to, Emory couldn't see why she would do it for him unless it was because he was a gentleman. He wouldn't even expect it if he could just travel the odor to its source at her throat.

Rawl leaned around and put his hand on Dode's shoulder. She turned to see who it was. Rawl made clown eyes. She looked away after stirring the air with a shrug that set her scent in motion. The door swung out and she went down the steps and away with the other girls. To inhale, Emory had to release the essence saved in his nose; he deferred the loss by breathing as lightly as he could to sustain life.

The girls crossed the road, angling toward the blacktop that led to Hillcrest Acres. Emory would have followed, but traditionally boys went home by the shortcut across the sandpit that had been dug down to a level field. At the far side they climbed the wall of the excavation and got to Hillcrest the back way. The boys crossed under the shelter of the flasher and stopped on the shoulder, taking a cue from Dex who wanted to see what kind of boat South Shore Transport was hauling.

Caught on the upgrade by the school-bus flashers, South Shore Transport was pissed; he would have to go through six gears to move his trailer to the marina.

Behind South Shore the pickup showing the flag of ISUZU estimated his chance of getting the jump and going around in the breakdown lane before the road narrowed at the underpass. The boys were in his way, lagging. ISUZU inched to the right to let them know he wanted them to move on, he was going through in the breakdown as soon as the bus released him.

Dex identified the boats. "Day Sailers."

The bus began to roll. The transport blatted diesel out of its periscope. ISUZU gunned and inched and honked the boys to get out of the breakdown lane.

"Stick it," Dex mouthed toward him. The words formed behind his lips and were not visible. He would have showed a finger, but the last time the guy drove off the road and came after him across the hardpan sand like a jackrabbit hunter in the movies, headed him off and chased him in a footrace, shoved him down running; stood over him looking like he might kick him with a cement-crusted workboot.

"Remember my face, you crud. Salute next time you see me," they guy had said.

This wasn't the face, but Dexter Reddick remembered. His ambition was to be big and tough enough someday to run into the guy again and show him the finger. He would break the guy. He would make him go down on his knees. On the English assignment *My Ambition* he wrote: "I would like to own an Imported Car Agnesy."

ISUZU gave up, left rubber on the road and went on, showing a finger in their faces. Dex thought it was safe to return the compliment as there was no way for ISUZU to turn around in the traffic and get back to him in a hurry. He stood on the shoulder showing Rawl and Emory that he dared ISUZU to come back; he would wait. When he concluded this statement he joined the others.

They walked into the bare fairgrounds that remained after a quarter century of digging at the sand hill. What was gone had sanded every icy road within twenty miles, and filled a hundred marshes before the law said they couldn't do that anymore.

As they walked they looked for valuables that might be left from the carnival. People reached into their pockets for combs, handkerchiefs, cigarettes, paper money; coins dribbled out. They dropped earrings, knives and ballpoint pens. Last year Rawl found among the blowing papers a change purse with eight dollars.

This year the town had read the riot act to the owners, threatened never to issue them a permit again unless they left the place as clean as they found it. The Board of Health man and the parks manager stood around yesterday to watch the carnival pack up and pull out. Not much had been overlooked: a pair of pliers, a big stove bolt, a couple of combs, a penny, a ping-pong ball, a fossil shell. Fossil shells were easy to find and had nothing to do with the carnival.

"This used to all be under the ocean," Emory said, looking up at the wash of high clouds. "This could have been a mile under."

"Help, I'm drowning!" Rawl began to swim desperately.

"Watch out for sharks!" Dex exclaimed. He showed his teeth in Emory's face. While he was that close he grabbed the ballpoint out of Emory's shirt pocket and held it behind his back when the slighter boy reached to retrieve it.

"Come on, that's a good pen," Emory said.

Rawl came around and picked off the pen as if it had been a baton in a relay race and trotted off with it. Emory knew he ought to be cool but couldn't take his own advice. Disabled by his book bag, he chased after Rawl. Dex came behind and took a handoff, and Emory chased after him, saying, "Come on, that's a good pen. That wasn't a freebie. Come on, I got that for a present." He was mad at them and mad at himself for not being cool but he was already into it and didn't know how to stop.

He knew it was going to end with Dex dangling the pen like a bob and offering it, and as soon as he reached Dex would let it fall. Emory prepared to come under it and catch it before it hit the ground and Dex kicked it away and he would have to chase it. He knew it would happen that way but he kept on after Dex as though he could take the pen from him.

Rawl left Emory to Dex. He ambled toward the cliff and the path that led up to their houses. Dex passed the pen from hand to hand behind his back while Emory tried to get his arms around to it. That just showed how stupid Emory was that he thought he could get his arms around and take anything from him that he didn't want to give up. Emory was trying to pin his arms. Jesus, he was dumb. Emory had his shoulder in Dex's chest and his can and legs were stretched back as if to give him leverage to make Dex give ground. What good would that do him? Dex had the whole field to back into.

Dex suddenly backed, pulling Emory with him off-balance. At the same time he brought around his left hand with the pen in it and grabbed Emory by his collar and lifted his face, and with his right hand he grabbed for Emory's dick. He caught him with an erection that had begun in the bus and raised again in the scuffle. Dex grinned into his face. "You want to fuck with me hey hey?"

Emory began to cry and pull away. Dex wouldn't let go. "Put it out, put it out hey hey."

Emory cried and begged, "Let go, let go, come on Dex, let go" in the mingled panic of discovery and desire for the exquisite process to go on. Dex released when he felt the leap and damp of the spill penetrate the cloth of Emory's jeans.

He wiped his hand on the front of Emory's shirt. "Here's your pen," he said. When Emory reached for it, he dropped it and kicked it away. He kicked it again when Emory went after it, and then he ended the game and let Emory have it.

Emory stood in silence, sniffling up the end of his sob, waiting for Dex to go on and leave him alone. The shame would follow him forever. It did not occur to him to wish a retaliatory pain. He wished only his tormentor's silence. He could think of nothing less than murder that would assure it.

Dex said, "Forget it. You're not hurt. That's nothing."

Rawl hollered from a short way ahead, "Look what's here."

"What have you got?" Dex hollered.

"They left a wagon."

"Come on," Dex motioned Emory. "Let's see." When Emory did not indicate that he was going along Dex said, "Don't be a baby. I promise I won't say anything."

That Dex realized he had something to say impressed Emory with his own helplessness. He had no means to enforce the promise.

"You go ahead."

"If you're going to stand here and feel sorry for yourself, the promise is off."

That's how good the promise was. It could be turned on and off. It would hang over him the rest of his life. Everybody would know it. Even girls would know it. He saw that his pants were stained and covered it with his book bag.

He decided he would be better off to go along with Dex, who then might not tell Rawl. He followed a few steps behind.

They came up to Rawl at the foot of the cliff in which erosions provided paths up and over. In a groin at the foot of the cliff, screened further by a scrubby growth of trees and bushes, a circus wagon tilted back on the haunch of a broken rear wheel, its tongue aimed outward in a posture of defense.

"They couldn't roll it. I'll bet they come back to get it," Rawl said.

Rust oozed through the white-painted iron rods that formed the wagon's sides. A rust-scarred iron door closed the back end. The rods were capped and footed with panels of wood, painted in scrolly red, white and green in which messages of various importance were emblazoned: *BANNISTER'S CARNIVAL . . . Featuring Louis Senti's Trained Wild Animal Show . . . Famous Worldwide . . . Rolling Stock #8. LION WAGON.*

"Aaaaaargh," Dex roared.

Rawl scrambled over the weedy uneven ground to the back and found the door closed by an unlocked hasp. He yanked the hasp free and the door fell open. He hauled himself in. He held onto a bar with one hand to balance himself on the teetered floor, scratched vigorously under his armpit in a confusion of identity between a lion and a gorilla, and echoed Dex's roar.

Dex came around and climbed in to share the experience of being caged. Both boys roared at Emory, "Aaaaaaaargh. Aaaaaaaargh."

Emory was satisfied to observe, but when they continued to prance around and roar he felt excluded. He saw a way to work himself into their favor. A broken two-by-four of good length to drag along the bars and make a noise lay on the ground. He banged his way to the back and got in with them. He continued to defend himself with his book bag.

They welcomed him with broad gestures, pointed insanely at each other and at him and at imaginary people and events outside, and continued to converse in their language.

"Aaargh."

"Argh aargh."

"Argh argh argh."

Emory made his way to the front of the cage, held onto the bars and addressed the universe. "Aaaargh. Aaaaargh." He imagined himself to be the MGM lion. "Aargh argh. The movie today is *Thirty Seconds Over Tokyo* argh argh." The mighty noise possible to make in this strange personality gave him a feeling of power. "Aaaaarrrgh. Starring Emory Wayne." He turned to see if they got it about MGM. They were jumping out the door.

Knowing he must be the butt of something he hustled to catch them, but they had too much of a lead and were out. They flung the door back and set the hasp before he could get there.

"Okay, guys," he said.

"Look at that dumb lion," Dex said.

"Yeah, what's he doing in there?"

"Yeah, what are you doing in there?"

The only thing Emory could think to say that would show he could take a joke and was in it with them was, "Aaaargh."

"You can't talk to a lion," Rawl said.

"Yeah, let's get out of here."

They began to walk away. "Okay, you guys," Emory said.

They began to climb the path. He thought he would show that he didn't give a damn and outwait them. The less fuss he made the sooner they would lose interest and come back. That's what his mother had said. "Don't fuss after them and they won't bother you."

He thought he might be able to get out without them. He reached his arm around the opening in the bars closest to the door to get at the hasp. He had the tip of his thumb on it, but the angle was awkward for leverage against the weight of the door falling back from the tilted wagon. He worked at the hasp. It wouldn't budge, he couldn't get enough finger under it.

They turned to look at him occasionally and kept going. Soon they were cut off by the angle of the roof. They were going farther than he thought they would want to return. He was sure Dex was telling the story about him coming in his pants, exaggerating it.

He shouted, "Come on, you guys, I've got to get home. Hey Dex! Rawl! Come on!"

He was suddenly overwhelmed by a suffocating sensation he had known before in crowded elevators and once even when he had been caught inside a sweater and couldn't find the opening to get his head out. His breath shallowed, he was irrationally scared.

He had heard of claustrophobia. He had thought he might have a touch of something like that, but it didn't happen often and it didn't happen to other people that he knew about, and he thought he would get over it. It didn't make any sense that other people could be in a crowded elevator without thinking about it, and he would feel that he couldn't breathe, he had to get out. It must be something he could work on, talk to himself about, get over.

Once he was in the Orleans Theater when the air conditioning broke down, and it was like a blanket coming down over him and he had to get out. The time a string caught on a button and wrapped around his arm for a few seconds, only a few seconds, terror surged in him. He knew in his head it was only a package string that constrained him, but he couldn't make his lungs understand, they wouldn't pump.

He felt himself suffocating, disintegrating and began to holler and cry and beat at the bars with his book bag.

They sat at the top of the hill, looking over the skirt of brush to the far edge of the fairground and the highway, waiting for him to catch up. They listened to his voice coming to them with the faintness of an echo and said to each other that he was dumb, maybe he was smart in school but he was dumb, all he had to do was reach around and throw the hasp and he would be out. When the voice stopped they expected he would be along, but he didn't show.

"He must have gone around on the blacktop," Dex said.

"I'm supposed to get home before my dad and cut the grass. I have to go."

"Okay. We better take a look first. He's really dumb."

They went down the path until they could see into the cage. He lay on the deck face down with his head on his arms and his papers scattered all around.

From the slope they called, "Hey stupid, reach around by the door, you can open the lock."

He didn't answer. He didn't move. He was playing a game back on them. At the same time an edge of feeling entered them that it might not be a game, something might be wrong. They couldn't account for the broken-open book bag and the papers thrown around.

They came down, talking to him—"Wake up, dumbhead. Come on out. Joke over. Jesus, we had to come all the way back to get you. Can't you see you can open the lock? What a dumb cluck."

They got around to the door and pulled the hasp loose and the door fell open.

He stirred and lifted his head to identify the source of the disturbance. He swung around to face them with the blank look of someone awakened.

"What are you doing in there, stupid?"

He rested on a hip and elbow and looked at them indifferently. He swung to his feet without haste. He walked slowly to the open door and studied the opening as if he needed permission to go through.

"Stay in there if you want."

He jumped down lightly.

It made them uneasy that he said nothing. They backed off. As they did he leaped at Dex, who turned to duck away. The two fell to the ground with Emory on top, his legs scissored around Dex's body, his arms binding him, and his head sunk into Dex's neck. He was growling and Dex screamed,

"Get him off! He's chewing on me! Get him off!"

Rawl pulled on Emory but couldn't budge him. He seemed to be welded on. Rawl was amazed at Emory's strength. He pounded on him with both fists until Emory lifted his head. His face was smeared with blood from Dex's torn and bleeding neck, a ferocious rumble came from his throat; when his eyes came around, Rawl saw they were yellow.

Rawl was going to run but was afraid to be a coward. He remembered the two-by-four Emory had rattled along the bars and went for it while behind him the *aaargh aaargh aaargh* and the screaming went on. He picked up the two-by-four, thinking what people would say. It made no difference, he had to do it. They would understand he just had to. He heard himself screaming too and he knew that as long as he made enough noise to smother his fear he would be able to swing the club.

Running Well

1

AFTER his first job in Altoona, Web Carey went to *The Post-Gazette* in Pittsburgh for eight years and then he was on *The Blade* in Toledo. He was assistant city desk on *The Philadelphia Bulletin* when liquor caught up with him. His editor Verne Bollard was a drayhorse of a man and had spongy places from his ankles to his ears where an extra shot could be stashed, but Carey was a jockey. What business had Carey to think he could drink with big men? Bollard talked to Carey. It didn't take. Once a month or so the assistant city editor had a day when he couldn't operate. It was getting to be two days, three days. It loused up the room.

The editor watched him sit at his typewriter with his hands on the keys. He didn't move. It went on for an hour. He thought Carey might stiffen in that position and die bent and there would be no way to bury him without breaking his bones. He talked to Carey's wife.

"It's only been the last few years," Bernice said. "He always drank more than he should but he could operate the next day fine. Since our second daughter married and there's only the two of us it's got so he can't handle it. Maybe it's me. He gets started and doesn't know when to stop and I can't stop him."

"It isn't you. You're what holds him together. He ought to give the AA's a whirl."

"He won't do it. He says he's not a drunk, he just drinks too much and he can stop anytime."

"Yeah. What would you think of this? If you can get him to take the cold-turkey deal at Coe Institute the paper will foot the bill."

"He won't do it."

"Check it out."

He wouldn't do it and he lost that job. Bernice thought she would have to give up on him after twenty-four years. All that investment, their youth, kids grown and gone, soon there would be grandchildren. After all those good years she would have to get a job that would last her to the end and let him work it out for himself.

"Is it that bad?" he asked. "You would really leave?"

"I'm in no hurry, but one more binge—and it won't be long, the way you're going—and I have to do it. I've got to make a life, Web. Where is your next job going to be?"

"There are jobs out there."

He hadn't answered her but he didn't want to say anything more on the spur of the moment. He hadn't thought through what he was about to say and was afraid to risk it. He let her go on telling him again what he was doing to himself and to her while he talked over in his head whether he should say it. He decided if he said it, then he would follow his own word.

"I've had my last drink."

"If I could believe it."

"You never heard me say it before."

"You're going to quit cold turkey?"

"I already did."

"When was that?"

"I haven't had a drink all day."

"I want to be a believer. You know that, Web. I want to be a believer."

"Believe what you see."

At the end of a month he said to her, "How would you like to live in a small town someplace in New England? We could have a garden, whatever that is."

"Have you got something lined up?"

"I'm looking for something."

Bernice said it was up to him, she always made friends pretty fast, and it would be nice being near the children and now a grandchild.

"Don't get us into one of those gloomy towns where the movie's out on the highway and there's only one church and the Witnesses."

Sam Kasper at the *Globe*, who had known him since Toledo, told him the *Cape Cod Fog* had an editor who appreciated a well-written story. A weekly like that usually hired kids, trained them for a year or two and let them go to a daily, but they had a core of veterans editing and writing features who wouldn't leave the Cape for money. They left only when they died.

Kasper said, "One of them must have known you were coming in to see me. It was on the wire this morning that Coop Kinney had his last heart attack. Coop wrote as good a three hundred words on any subject as anybody you can name. It'll take a real writer to replace him. If you want, you can use my name down there." He reached into a pile of newspapers on the desk behind him. "Here. You can get acquainted. Keep it."

On the *Fog* he did what came up—Town Hall, water pollution, lost cats. He developed a regular column of people-pieces that was well-received. One of the pieces worked up into a short story. He thought it was pretty good, but nobody would publish it, and he wrote another that nobody published. He wrote a half dozen stories before a Canadian magazine bought one. He was then in his middle fifties.

The story that established him was "The Coprophagiasts." No magazine would touch a story like that, but you can put anything in a book. He tucked it into his first collection. It was the story every review mentioned, the reason they paperbacked it. "The Coprophagiasts" established Web Carey as a writer nothing could faze. He wrote in a low key, one sentence after another, the way he covered a meeting of the Board of Selectmen. It could have been signed by one of those English craftsmen who flourished between the World Wars, before first-person-present tense was discovered.

Nobody would have thought Carey's story was anything but a good *A Day in the Life of*— if it had been about an alcoholic or a junkie, as no one would have thought anything if the Portnoy kid hid in the bathroom to smoke a cigarette. Those were established vices. But it wasn't cigarettes and it wasn't masturbation ten years later, it was coprophilia, and whether you wrote about heavy smokers or drunks or Portnoy or the dung-ho couplings of Jorge Merdenger and Celia Ghooste, you had to tell it piece by piece, nobody got credit anymore for what he didn't say. A man went to certain places, he was involved with certain people who did specific acts. Carey's story took people into that world.

Bernice read it and said, "This is disgusting. This is unspeakable."

"I was afraid you were going to say it was indescribable."

After that Bernice occasionally looked at Web when he wasn't looking at her. Such an unobtrusive, agreeable companion, who didn't mind going to the supermarket with her Saturday mornings—

People asked where did he get an idea like that for a story? As if the world were anything but stories.

"From a man who sat next to me in church."

"He told you the story in church?"

"He leaned over and asked me the hymn number. I don't know who he was." A hundred years ago Henry James said that was all he wanted, any more distracted him.

His second collection didn't have anything as gutty as that but it didn't need it. The story had released something in him so that whatever he wrote had a quality of disclosure. The stories came forward as well-researched journalism, well-observed, written at leisure.

He took his stories where he found them (never bothered by it, Shakespeare did too) and looked around the supermarket or the post office for the characters he needed. He had to see the person in front of him as he wrote—the fall of the hair, the edge of the hairline, how the brow flexed, how little it took to narrow his eye, how fast he ate, how he changed when speaking to different auditors. It made their friends a little uneasy that he might take that snapshot and put them in a story that used only the parts they themselves liked characters in stories to have, the worst.

The Careys had two daughters, one married unexceptionably to a steady man, a dentist. The profession had become a shorthand to express amused disdain, but it was Web's observation that dentists as a class were more accountable for performance than sufficiently-honored physicians and had a larger investment in the machinery of their trade. The specific dentist Selwyn Gates, who was his son-in-law, had every virtue a father could wish for Agnes. He was solvent, his intelligence was quick, his interest in the world broad. He was an attentive and imaginative husband and father.

Louise had not done as well as Agnes. That marriage was now twelve years of disappointment, stress and make-do while Paul, an assertive man with a core of apology, went from salesman in an art-supply store to opening and closing a pottery shop to being a fence salesman to his present partnership in another pottery shop. That would blow up in another year or so, Web supposed, sitting in his lounge chair, watching the family—Bernice, five grandchildren, Ag and Norm, Lou and Paul—beginning to disperse to the TV, board games, head-to-head talk after the first Thanksgiving dinner together in years.

He watched Lou's boy grab the marble game from Ag's second; grabbed it roughly and stared at her to do something about it. His eyes glittered. With that back-sloped head of his father, he was reptilian. Mary turned away from confrontation.

Louise came over and pulled up the footstool. She was smoking a cigarette, as he was. They were the only two smokers left in the family. He thought she was a stitch tight in her clothes.

"Good party, Pop."

"It's good to have everybody in one room. Everybody looks okay. How are things in your house?"

"We're normal for us. You seem to be having a good year. You even got a review in Worcester. I sent it to you."

"I got it. Thanks. It might sell three books."

She drew in smoke to the pit of her stomach and said, "That's better than two," before the smoke began to come out.

"You shouldn't inhale that deep."

"We shouldn't inhale at all . . . Pop, you wouldn't do anything like put my family in a story, would you?"

"I never thought of it."

"If you thought of it would you do it?"

She had a lot of grainy gray hair mixed in the brown now. She pinched her lower lip between her thumb and ring finger, and narrowed her eyes against the drift of smoke.

"Do you want me to?"

"I'd kill you if you did."

"In that case it wouldn't be a good idea."

"You go into the lives of people like God. Do you ever tell it exactly like it is or do you always mix and match so it's this person but somebody else's story? Like in the gambler story—"

He gave her the name of the story.

"Yes. Was it those people who did that or was it different people in that story? Do you know what I'm talking about?"

"That happened to be a couple I know. I picked up the story somewhere. I don't remember where. It might have been something I heard on the radio."

"If I had been that woman I would have killed you even if the story was made up."

"Really? Why?"

"You made it her story. You described her to a T, then you gave her that awful thing to do. If people around town knew who she was, they would think it was her story. I would have killed you."

He laughed. "You'd kill you own father for something like that?"

"I think I really would. My family is that important to me. You would kill for Mother, wouldn't you?"

He kept laughing. "You're a tough case. I'm glad I don't

have many readers like you. I would have to write children's stories."

The conversation bothered him and stayed with him when dusk fell and the families said goodbye and drove off for their homes in Worcester and Wayland.

He had come to feel enormously potent in his work, like an athlete in perfect condition running well. He sat down to his typewriter every morning with a hunger to begin and the certainty that the work would run successfully to its appointed or discovered end, with every intervening block yielding to the onslaught of his fingers on the keys. That there might be a paragraph he could not enter, a story he could not tell on peril of anyone's displeasure or even of his life, diminished his dominion over his work.

It was especially troubling that the challenge was raised by Lou, his favorite between the daughters and, at the time he thought her in a bad season—losing control of her life—favored as the vulnerable are favored.

Ag went unerringly to the right boyfriend, the right major, the right husband, and bred praiseworthy kids. Lou always found the struggling side of things. She would go up the wrong side of a mountain. God, the boyfriends she schlepped, the husband she chose. The children—one after the other whiny, wild—with unloving, self-centered natures written all over their faces; and Lou would lay down her life for them.

One had to love one's own blood who got up in the morning to kids and a husband like that, and say she would kill you if you wrote it. Maybe not with a gun but she would kill what was between father and daughter. He wished Lou was as clean of problems as Ag but wishes had nothing to do with it.

Carey brought the reflection with him to lunch with his agent in Boston. They went to the seafood house people were talking about. He didn't drink so she took the cue and didn't either, she didn't want to do anything that hampered the flow.

They had just begun to talk about the contract when he was served. It was as if the chef had been standing with a wrong order and the waiter had done him a favor and taken it off his hands. Her order they seemed to have thrown away. Web fiddled with his food while they waited and looked around and motioned at their waiter who looked everywhere else; tried what looked like a senior waiter, and a manager, and spent the better part of the course discussing what difference did it make how famous was the chef and what schools he had attended if nobody paid any attention to a table where two people ordered from the same entrée list and one was served and the other just sat, mad as hell. They reached an understanding about the contract while his subconscious idled through a story about a diffident woman who starved to death in a famous restaurant.

Before the day ended, anxious to be away from a disaster in which only he knew his degree of complicity, the waiter shoved a plate at her, said something half irrational, half unintelligible, and got away, and Carey was relieved of the duty to be concerned. He said, "Not to interfere with your well-deserved lunch, but when you get a chance tell me—do you think any subject is barred to a writer?"

"Yes. One he can't pull off," she said around a chunk of salmon.

"But if you can do it, you have a right to it, don't you?"

"I should think you had not only a right but a duty to reach for your limit." A shame they knew so much about cooking and so little about running a dining room. "Why, has something come up?"

He ignored the question. "Right belongs to me. But duty— to whom?"

She had not expected to be back at Goucher in a dormitory bull session on account of an innocent remark. "To your art. You owe it to Balzac and Roth and your children to go all the way."

"I owe it to my children?"

"Posterity." She was afraid she sounded heavy. "What are

you working on? You make it sound intriguing." Let him answer the questions, she had half a plate to go.

2

For Web and Bernice Carey it was the best part of the year. The heat was over, the checkout aisles quickly cleared. Like Bemmelmans' children, the quail marched from the woods, and Nurse Clavel stood watch while they scratched up corn outside the kitchen window. An oak had leaves the color of raspberries, a maple turned so yellow it had to be fake. They had a garden, and their first cantaloupes ever that came sweet.

They were up and ready for the day at sunrise. She put the house together, shopped, gave three mornings to the hospital branch and one to retarded readers. He worked on stories. After lunch they waded out to their rattle-boat parked off Town Landing, and rattled down the river into the bay while he dressed the poles and she steered and throttled.

They spoke of the landscape and were silent and fished. They spoke of the children and were silent and fished. They spoke of friends who were coming to visit, friends who were hospitalized, a newspaper that had been sold to a chain, what the president had said yesterday. They found flounder. They rattled home. He gutted the fish for dinner and the freezer.

When the evening chill settled in, he thought that an inch of bourbon on a night like this surely couldn't do any damage, surely he had enough character not to let it go any farther; but he knew he didn't and willed to forget it.

He reflected on problems that were beyond human means to address and those that lay within the will. Almost every interesting problem yielded to will. There had only to be enough will. Yet there eternally was not enough will, a lack that also must be a problem beyond human means; a natural law that decreed the effective will to be ineffective, as the law of crowds was different from the law of persons. Seldom could anybody use all the will he knew he had.

She said, "You look like you're getting ready to lay an egg. What are you brooding about?"

"I'm trying to take two clauses out of a sentence."

He went for a walk alone, intending only to make the circle around the church and back while he pondered the problem of the power and vulnerability of the will, and what determined the brink from which it must continually recede. He went farther than he intended and, passing The Landing Bar, went in to experience his will ending at the bar. He did not succeed, but he had the satisfaction of knowing he had taken one and stopped. And taken another and stopped. Definitely stopped, he could get up and walk away.

The crowd at the bar was young, as if a second exclusionary I.D. kicked in around thirty-five. He was twice as old as anybody there. Because he had gotten around as a newspaperman, he knew a few of the youngsters and a few more knew him. He had no conversation for any of them, only a nod and yes he was enjoying the weather.

A chubby Asian woman wearing feminist steel rims, sitting on a stool, talking to a man, made a sudden cutting motion with the side of her hand. He wondered what had been said with the motion and began to inventory her from her dungareed legs, crossed, full and shapeless as fish sticks. A man's dungaree jacket with the cuffs turned back; the front hung open and showed a rope belt with a jailer's key ring. Not the man she talked to; he was the wrong size for her jacket.

Walking home he thought further what the motion of the hand under the turned-up cuff might mean or be made to mean when an Asian woman in man's clothing talked to a man not her husband at a bar on Cape Cod. The Asian woman had his daughter's legs. She didn't have to be Asian. She could have been his daughter talking to her husband about the children, telling him she had a new life with an Asian woman, cutting him off with a gesture. An Asian woman, an interesting relationship.

Only the living-room watch light was on. Bernice was in bed. He had not been gone long enough for her to be asleep.

She was reading. For no specific reason, merely the sight of her looking up from the book, he thought: how well she kept the compact for better or worse, and it had worked out. He had eaten pretzels and mints and smoked but was sure the odor of liquor remained on his breath and that he dare not kiss her goodnight.

He said, "I have some work to do. I'll be awhile."

He went into his den and rolled a sheet of paper into the Smith-Corona in which alphabets had been battered and replaced while he fought it for stories. He said to himself: Nothing has precedence over art. The edge at which he met the demands of art—recalcitrant and beckoning—was the outermost reach to which his will extended. He felt his authority over the instrument. He wrote:

. . . *The tide of life moved toward Martin, he drifted in it, taking hold of nothing. To berate him was to berate a phlegm of jellyfish (a phlegm—ah!) bobbing in the shallows. What had made her bet her life on this agreeable man who could not close his hand on a job, on a dollar, on fatherhood? He had been born without a nerve connecting his will to the muscles of his fingers, and she had been a fool to think that if she said often enough Why don't you? and What if? and Please for God's sake! that she could make him go.*

Carey was into the third page and running well; passing assenters to creaturely habit and devised law, seeing himself there; passing husbands, wives, mothers, fathers in contractual huddles against insidious, abominable, time-bound fates, seeing himself among them; running well toward the beckoning muse, the only possible ultimate reason and salvation.

If that had to be proved, how better than with the most formidable love of his life at stake?

. . . *He said "What about the kids? I want my kids."*

She swirled the drink and saw there was enough left to get her to the end of the conversation. She took in a bellyful of smoke and held it like a man while she pinched her lip between her thumb and ring-finger and considered his question. The impulse to show her contempt was too strong to resist. "Take them."

He groped for a way to deal with the incomprehensible answer. "You want me to take the kids?"

What she wanted and what had to happen were not the same. Of course the kids would be hers, it was the way the world worked. She had another ten years of penance for her mistake. She would try and fail to be the nerve between the will of the child and the failing grasp while Kevin dropped out and stole cars and knocked up girls and Laura dropped out and moved in with a boy who made salad bowls and drugged whatever were the smokes and pills of the times. Ten years and she would be free.

She relented. "I don't want them, but they come to me, it's the way things are." She signaled the bartender who came over to find out about refills. "You don't want them. You want to talk about wanting them. You want to talk about everything."

"You've got a fat lip and a fat ass."

The answer had bite but no substance, it was his act of bravado that made him feel that he counted too, like other men. It was a line he had heard in a movie and recited to put himself in a part. She chopped him off with a karate stroke that cut between them. "So we get out of each other's lives. I get the kids and the check? Right?"

A Marriage Kind of Secret

BEING able to say what happened on the job today is a small pleasure an ordinary man has that is denied a burglar. The event itself may be insignificant, but the telling is of another life in which minds are faster, tongues quicker, strange characters are met, rare objects handled, heroism experienced. A lieutenant of Arthur's court patrolling the lesser suburbs all day in an iron suit looked forward to pulling up a siege to the roundtable, throwing back a mead, and bidding for the respect of his peers: "I'm grailing in Druid Woods south of the Avebury roundabout when I see this giant green knight. I don't mean his uniform, I mean *him*. Green . . ."

With whom can Dell Beelauck share his adventures? South Westham has two societies of Knights, several orders celebrating antlered and fanged beasts, Masons, two veterans' halls, a country club, a grange, an AA, friends of libraries and hospitals, houses of worship beyond census, and three lots of fellows odd and otherwise (now, since the Troubles, including four or five women) who assemble for lunch at hours shown on The Quarterdeck Restaurant sign at the entrance to town; but it has no Brotherhood of Burglars. Beelauck cannot mention his moonlight job to anyone at Dowling's or Ship Ahoy Tavern. He can't mention it to Pam as he is not that tightly married.

He doesn't even know what he knows until he reads it in the leftover newspaper on Dowling's counter: *Mrs Walker Woodforth was brutally slain in her home on Bastorf Lane in a secluded area of Brewster Wednesday night when she apparently surprised an intruder.*

He can't tell Speed Canaday sitting next to him reading the leftover sport page; or Linda smearing the counter clean with a rag; or Dowling brooming up floor dust to settle in quiet defiance of the Board of Health on cinnamon, chocolate, honey-glaze, raised, sugar, cruller, plain and jelly-belly.

He can't tell anybody all day, and when he gets home he can't tell Pam, so he tells her what happened on his real job behind the counter of Westham Auto Parts and she doesn't give a damn.

She keeps her head down over the sink, watching herself rinse dishes. A big-framed stolid man, he speaks in a slow word-by-word drone. "You know Gosslinger? From the Texaco? Do you know him or don't you know him? How would I know if you don't say? He came in today asking for the new 326C7 filter. I told him it was out but the old 290R fitted just as well. Goose wouldn't believe me, but I told him to try it. If it didn't fit bring it back. He never came back. People don't know how things work anymore, they just know numbers. Gosslinger is supposed to be a mechanic. He gets fourteen dollars an hour but he doesn't know parts."

His Filter #326C7 speech seems to Pam to take as long as Friday morning at the supermarket.

Who would tell a woman like that about the other job?

They are more or less forty, a second marriage and several live-ins on for both, and neither seems to have learned much about how such joint ventures are made to work. She is often attractive; a little sodden, but she can put herself together to go to a movie or The Shingles, and can produce a smile of utter delight in which her eyes glisten and her face is disarmed of wariness. He has not seen her so disarmed for two or three years.

"I have to meet somebody," he says. "I won't be late."

She doesn't ask where he is going or who it is or why. If she asks he'll tell her Ship Ahoy, Fritz Dart, Speed Canaday, he's dickering on an outboard.

She wouldn't believe him anyhow. He must be seeing a woman. Still, it is a matter of pride that now and then she grunt or crease her forehead in derision to let him know she is not dumb.

She creases her forehead. "I may walk over to Marie's if she's home. If I'm not here when you get back."

He believes her. He doesn't think she is seeing a man; if she were it would blow things open. A man can't have it known that his wife sees another man. Even thinking about the possibility stimulates anger in which Beelauck assumes the personality of a large animal to whom it would be futile to say, "Come, let us reason together."

Pam runs the counter at Repin's Dry Cleaning and Laundry, so she has her own money, but one wage doesn't get anywhere these days, and Dell is clean and has a pretty good overdrive and is not rough. Between his eight dollars an hour and her six they make $29,000 a year, not bad until the government takes. There hasn't been a house for sale in any of the Westhams since 1980 that a bank will agree they can afford.

Now and then she meets the man who has the route for the linen company and they go to his room in Brewster. She knows he'll never settle down with another woman so it's no use moving over to him. She and Repin's brother-in-law sometimes encounter each other behind the trolley rows of finished garments and exchange heat, but that is mostly so she can see how jazzed-up he gets over nothing at all. She doesn't go any further than breaking him off as a favor while they stand there.

Dell doesn't fool around with other women; no, he wouldn't say he did. He may leave the bar with somebody and they get in his pickup and drive to the hardware parking lot, but there is nobody he sees regularly.

He owns the truck and a power mower and every couple of years he puts an ad in the paper that a reliable man does yard work, cleans out attics, makes dump runs. He gets in a few hours of odd jobs after work and on weekends. These enterprises peter out. Customers want things done at the wrong time or won't pay a fair price or expect too much. It comes down to running the ads in order to have addresses on a piece of paper that give him a reason to drive around Private Citizen Watch neighborhoods with a mower in the back of the pickup looking for houses to rob, which is how he happened to be at Walker Woodforth's that night.

Mrs Woodforth called about the ad. She asked if he could come over and talk about turning over a garden. A couple of trees might have to be taken down. "No, Wednesday evening would not be a good time to come, my husband and I are going to dinner and a concert in Hyannis, but anytime Saturday." Would he be sure to come? She didn't want to start in with anybody who says he will come and doesn't.

"People who know me know I keep my word," he said. "I'll be there at ten A.M. Saturday morning."

After dinner Wednesday he told Pam he had to see somebody. He put on an Army & Navy Store windbreaker and blue watch cap. From behind his bundle of foul weather gear he took the .38 they had torn Camp Kilmer apart looking for when it was missed from an officer's desk drawer. It was a clunk weapon that went with World War I photos of Pittsburgh iron mills. He hoped to replace it someday with a weapon more like the Japanese binoculars he picked up at the camera store. The windbreaker pocket made a neat holster when the barrel slid through the hole in the bottom.

After his lights disappeared on the road she looked to see if he took the gun while he was roughing up the closet. He must think she was too dumb to know. Who did he think cleaned up the house? If he was in on the marijuana runs they said were coming off the outer beach there ought to be signs of more money than the few dollars he showed when he said he won on the Patriots.

She wished he would tell her what was going on because that way they would be more together. Secrets shared between people did more to keep them together than splitting the rent and shacking up. She thought of women he might one day just as well split the rent and shack up with if he didn't have a marriage kind of secret with her. She turned it around to compare her options. She didn't like them.

He drove out Chatham Road to the off-season darkness of Westham Marine and parked far in, behind a cradled work-boat. A ridge buffered the sound of cars running the high-way. He sat at the wheel waiting for the canopy of town light reflecting from the clouds to resolve the landscape into shrub-bery humps and glacial boulders. Blue-fly and mosquito traps paraded through the cranberry bog like shrouded heads on poles.

He found the dry path that always lay close against a bog. His cleated shoes leveled ground frozen in hard lumps like manure. He carried two bags that once held horse feed. The path took him into a margin of pine trees that shed branches as they grew and intervened like a field of telephone poles between him and the house light. They must be city people to let scratch pines stand northeast, that close to the house; dead in forty years, dead of beetles sooner, limbs flying in every gale. Some windy night a sixteen-inch tree drilled out by beetles would split their roof. He worked his way until he stood in the trees off the front window.

Beelauck was upset to see through the slats of the blind a man and a woman at separate lamp tables, their backs to him, apparently reading. They were not supposed to be there. They were supposed to be in Hyannis for dinner and then a concert. His uninstructed hand brushed toward the gun pocket. He stepped back into the cover of woods before the instinct to protect himself accepted the reassurance of com-mon sense that he remained hidden.

He mulled whether to come back another night or wait until they went upstairs to bed. He didn't like the idea of people being upstairs with a telephone.

He pulled off a glove, tucked it into the pocket with the revolver, blew his fingers warm, and took the subcompact Nikon binocular from the other pocket.

In the glass everything was enormously enlarged, as if he sat in the first row at a movie. He looked into the eyes of a jury of face mugs sitting in a row on the top shelf of the bookcase. He read the brass instruments: clock, barometer, thermometer, windspeed. In a cabinet were porcelain figures that collectors paid a lot of money for. The kitchen would have an electric can opener. Toaster oven. Mixer. His dealer in Braintree liked things with wires.

They were older people, neither of imposing size. The man snapped his newspaper to get the crease out. The woman lighted one cigarette off another; Beelauck couldn't remember ever seeing a woman do that before. There didn't seem to be a dog.

The woman got up and crossed the room to the bookshelf.

As she did, the man reached to the side of the window and flicked the string of the blind. It did not quite close, one slat remained cocked. Beelauck saw at a rising angle from eye level in the middle of the room to the shelf of mugs.

While he adjusted to the new view an object swung across it. He was not prepared to see something in motion so high in the room. The object passing through the strobed gap in the blind appeared to be the man's arm, and his hand with something bright in it, describing an arc. The action was far more energetic than Beelauck expected in that room at that hour.

He did not understand what was going on but felt he would be better off somewhere else.

2

Walker Woodforth failed to anticipate that there would be physical consequences to himself as well as to his wife after he struck her. Weakness near fainting drained him. His arm shook. He began to doubt his strength. He had never before done anything more violent than shout at the driver of another car. He thought he too might be caught here, dead of a heart attack, the story plain enough with the two of them on the floor.

He was all right in a moment, breathing heavily but his mind clearing. She was slumped oddly against the bookcase, her cheek caught and turned sideways by the jut of the bottom shelf. He was profoundly thankful that she was unconscious and did not see him raise the electric iron to strike her again. He put her arm to her face, as though she tried to protect herself, and smashed the iron down again. It was necessary to do that to establish the crime as one that a man like Walter Woodforth could not even imagine committing. First he had thought of a gun, but anybody might use a gun. It would have to be hidden quickly nearby. What was hidden could be found.

Now there should be no improvisation of what had been so carefully planned. He had read that the ruin of criminals was to improvise under stress what they had not thought necessary beforehand. He dropped the iron to the floor, stuffed back into his pocket the handkerchief with which he had held it, went into the kitchen and cracked the door an inch. He switched on the upstairs hall light, took another look around and went up.

He sat on the edge of his bed, exhausted, and looked at his watch; seven minutes after nine. He thought that if anything proved he was not a criminal by nature it was this emotional exhaustion. He took off his tie and opened his collar. He took off a shoe. When the police came he would still have a shoe off, a realistic touch.

He had not known her quite well enough when they married, and discovered too late the spendthrift nature under her cover of a good sport. Having required them to move out of the city because it had become unsafe, dirty and noisy, she would not settle down in this quiet, satisfactory house she had herself chosen. She drove twenty miles on stormy nights to hear lecturers and string quartets, needed cleaning women, went on shopping sprees that peopled every shelf with gimcracks. She had begun to talk about moving to Florida. She couldn't get through her head that they lived where they were, on a modest income in unexpectedly inflationary times, that it cost money to cut down trees so flowers could be planted—and now another bathroom, for guests.

"Forty-six hundred dollars for a room that might be used a few times a year?"

"Oh, you add up everything. How much, how many. I don't know about you but I'd use it instead of trotting upstairs every time. Our friends shouldn't have to go upstairs to go."

"People won't stop visiting you because there isn't a bathroom on the first floor."

"You aren't sensitive to those things. Do you visit anybody who doesn't have at least a lavatory downstairs?"

His first wife had been a childhood neighbor and in marriage she remained the most undemanding person he had known. From that he supposed he was a judge of wives, and the woman lying on the floor downstairs had taken advantage of him. If his first wife had not had a bad heart they would have gone on together to the end, he would not have had to take a job again at his age, he would not be in anything like this.

His cold hands flexed with difficulty. He looked at his watch. He called out, "Marjorie? Marjorie? Did you call me?" and hurried to her—to be stunned by the sight; to dial first for the Rescue Squad, as he naturally would, thinking of her welfare. He asked them to tell the police, as he must return to his wife to see if there was anything he could do for her. He brought towels to deal with the blood, now considerable, and a pillow off the sofa; all in the order an overwrought husband would go about it before he went to the front door, pulled it open, and hollered "Help! Help!"—which Dell Beelauck heard not as words, but a wail all the way across the bog as he was getting into the Datsun.

To the police Woodforth was as helpful as a man in his position could be. They would find no reason to suspect him. Her insurance was no more than enough for a funeral. There was no other woman; although occasionally tempted, Woodforth thought another woman would certainly be an unaffordable expense. He described the ordinariness of the evening, going upstairs, the sounds that at first alerted then alarmed him; rushing down to find her battered on the floor, and the iron; telephoning the Rescue Squad, the effort to make her comfortable with the pillow but not do unknowing damage. He still wore only one shoe, evidence of his distraction. He had left the discovery of the open kitchen door to them.

"You didn't hear anything else after you got upstairs?"

"Just what sounded like something heavy dropping—and then she didn't answer when I called."

"The iron was always on the shelf in the kitchen? Show me how that would be."

Woodforth repeated for the assistant district attorney the testimony he had already given Lieutenant of Detectives Lestage, and when, a week later, Lestage asked him to visit headquarters to go over it again, Woodforth took satisfaction from the simplicity of the events he related. Lestage was obtuse, asked if he might talk to him at home still again. Woodforth caught himself repeating phrases identical with those used previously—*and not do unknowing harm in any way by moving her*—and thought it might sound rehearsed; fake?

The bereaved was intimidated by the detective's presence which was aggressive even when at rest. It seemed to Woodworth, who was of conventional size, weight and momentum, that Lestage was restless for a man so big. He picked up things, put his head aslant, sat sideways on the edge of chairs, shrugged as if constantly enlarging an invisible hole he lived in. His forehead sloped downward and his jaw upward in support of an aggressive nose, and even the natural marcel rippling back from his forehead seemed to be the consequence of the detective's forward impulse.

Lestage asked if there wasn't an insurance policy somewhere that had been overlooked. Lestage asked if he usually went upstairs and left it to his wife to put out the lights and lower the thermostat. "Why did he hit her twice? What would be the reason?" Lestage mused sideways as if the husband of the deceased could be expected to know the answer, and again looked at the windows and the doors and the placement of the furniture.

The unreasonableness of these inquiries annoyed Woodforth, as Lestage had not by any impeaching discovery earned the right to them.

Would an educated man of modest size and strength kill his own wife with an electric iron, a weapon of opportunity a brutish criminal had obviously seized in a fit of improvisation?

Did it make sense to keep after an attentive husband who went to church frequently with his wife, and only the night before the tragedy had gone with her to Hyannis to hear the Cape Cod Symphony?

Woodforth saw this busywork by the police as an inefficient use of manpower at a time they wanted to add twenty-three points to the tax bill for the department. He didn't say it to anyone but he resented the police budget being dissipated with so little imagination.

To the contrary—Lestage should be on another tack altogether. They had found a glove in the woods—who knows where that came from!

As Woodforth reflected about the glove it assumed conclusive importance. The glove was real leather with a wrist-strap and a separate slip-in wool liner. The mate surely was in a drawer in somebody's house. No man would be in any hurry to concede he had lost such a good glove forever. It took time to get used to the idea that a lost glove wouldn't ever turn up. Later on a man would tell himself that someday he would get another pair like the old one and have a spare. That's the way people thought, and Lestage didn't give it proper weight.

Lestage said a dog might have carried it from somewhere. That's what passed for police work.

Lestage in fact had the glove in his pocket at the moment along with an oddly shaped key and several photographs, all pertaining to cases he was working on. He had shown the glove in restaurants and gone up and down the bars with it and the only result was that Dell Beelauck put the other one in a hot fire in his woodstove.

Lestage found out that Monte Gordon's store stocked that number. Monte was even able to make his computer give up the name of a customer who had charged a pair: Ken Loeber at Dime Savings. Ken still had his. While Gordon was searching he found that he was short a pair that wasn't in stock and had never been sold, it had walked out the door.

A young reporter from the newspaper interviewed Wood-forth, nodding her head in a friendly way at what he had to say. Her article described the event as something "he said" — over and over again "he said" and "the husband of the deceased woman said" — and by this very precision opened a slight gap that admitted other possibilities. Even to say "he said they came from Hartford" implied that he might have lied about it; maybe they came from New Haven, as if he were not exactly forthcoming about where he lived before.

The statement that "Mr Woodforth said this was a second marriage, the first Mrs Woodforth having died of a heart attack" seemed to him unnecessary. It came out as one more curiosity about himself. Most people in the church did not even know about a previous marriage. He would be thought of as a man who had lost two wives in an untimely way. They would joke that Walker Woodforth's wives were not good insurance risks.

He thought he detected among people he knew a slight reserve that implied that by surviving he had neglected his duty as a husband. He had failed to be in harm's way sufficiently to engage the assailant and be severely injured, to give chase, to furnish a description. He foresaw that people would lose track, would identify him as — wasn't Woodforth the man whose wife was murdered in unresolved circumstances?

It was in the power of the police to make clear that Walker Woodforth was absolved of all suspicion, that they were looking for the owner of the glove, and Lestage had not rendered him that simple justice.

3

Woodforth stands at the Customer Service Desk studying a customer's check and driver's license brought to him by a saleswoman. He is the assistant service manager at Rogerson's, the big store in the mall. He came to the Cape thinking he was retired until his wife's profligacy and this new inflation — something he had thought of as a just visitation on Germans and Latin Americans — warned him that he might outrun his pension from the box company and his social security.

Had he come to Cape Cod with hand tools in his knapsack he would have found work at a good wage, but an eldering man looking for a dignified white-collar job competed in a large labor pool for low wages he spent at list price. The store felt especially lucky in getting Woodworth, a sober man in this land of long winters where men were not motivated to stop at one drink. He had not missed a day of work until the shocking tragedy. Everybody commiserated with him and hoped he would go on as before.

He initials his approval and turns to a husky man in a bombardier jacket who stands by to be acknowledged.

"Do you want to see me?"

Beelauck says in a confidential voice. "You're Woodforth?"

"Yes?" He has cultivated a brisk manner of speaking and an open countenance to overcome a mood of apprehension he blames on the unreasonable inquiries of Detective Lestage.

"I want to talk to you."

"Go right ahead."

"I want eighteen hundred dollars."

How can one respond to such a statement: who doesn't?

"I saw you kill your wife."

"Sir!" Woodforth exclaims, not suppressing his indignation. "Do you know what you're saying?"

"I was behind the big tree by your front window. I saw you. I want eighteen hundred bucks."

"Do you know what you're saying?" Woodforth demands

again. "I'll call the police and you can tell them." He inclines his body toward the telephone on the other end of the counter.

The man's stare dares him.

Woodforth is invaded by weakness, a feeling to which he has become accustomed in the months of rising and receding and again rising threats to his security. He suspects that he is in a serious discussion but he has heard nothing that requires him to admit it. He parries. "Who are you?"

"What difference does it make? Before you hit her you closed the blind, but you didn't close it all the way."

Woodforth's face enacts amazement at hearing an incredible story for the first time. Beelauck speaks to him as one felon to another. "Your wife got up and turned her back. You closed the blind and hit her. You know I know what I'm talking about. It's going to cost you eighteen hundred dollars. You're getting off cheap."

"What were you doing at my house?"

"That's nothing to you. I'm telling you what you did. You know I was there. That's all you need to know."

Beelauck has thought a great deal about how the money is to be handed over. He has considered the usual maneuvers of ransom payment—notes and masked telephone calls instructing Woodforth to stash it somewhere, or arranging to overtake Woodforth driving slowly on a back road. Not until last night did he see how simple it could be. This was not a ransom situation in which he was at risk of disclosure by the other party. He could just ask Woodforth to hand over cash.

However, Woodforth would not be able to take that much money out of his pocket, and a prearranged transfer of cash introduced a risk. Woodforth might think of a stunt to pull. If they met in an out-of-the-way place, a man who killed once might kill twice. If they met again in the store there could be some kind of stakeout. How could he pass off being handed all that cash?

This morning an idea both novel and obvious reassured him he was nobody's fool. The thing to do was get a check.

Handle it like any other check. He told himself that Woodforth called him last week to come by and look at the job and meet him at the store and give him an estimate. Woodforth gave him a down payment. Before that he didn't know Woodforth from Adam. They could ask Pam.

On the way to Hyannis he went over it again line by line, practicing what to say if something went wrong. He practiced "I didn't know him from Adam." He practiced "You can ask my wife."

"Make out a check for eighteen hundred dollars." Might as well give his name, he'll have to endorse it for the bank anyhow. "Make it to D. Beelauck. Write on it 'Down payment for tree work.'"

The purpose sounds right, and so does the amount. At first he intended to ask for five thousand dollars, but eighteen hundred is more convincing, and he can come back for more.

"I don't have that kind of money in the bank."

"How long will it take you?"

Woodforth does not want to indicate a date. He does not want to suggest even that he can get his hands on that much money.

"Write the check. I'll hold it three days. Go ahead before I raise the ante. I haven't got all day." Woodforth puts his checkbook on the counter. "Beelauck. B E E L A U C K." Nobody ever gets it right.

Woodforth does as he is instructed. Beelauck reminds him to write "Down payment for tree work."

"If you come back and try to get more I'll know who you are," Woodforth warns him. "You won't get away with it."

"Big mouth son of a bitch."

Beelauck's eyes, while looking downward in a conventional way as the escalator descends, are disconnected from his attention which remains on Woodforth, imagines him standing in irate frustration. He brushes his hand inconspicuously across the front of his jacket, feeling the hard shape of the gun. At other times it has been reassuring; now he doesn't know what it is there for. He is walking around with the I.D. of a criminal in his pocket. His attention turns from Woodforth on the floor above to getting into the pickup and driving away from there.

When the escalator carries the blackmailer below the floor line Woodforth goes to the phone and speaks urgently. "This is Woodforth. Get me Security fast." To Security he says, "This is Woodforth. A big man, over six feet, is coming off the escalator on main. Pick him up. He's wearing an old army type windbreaker, brown pants and a navy watch cap. He may be dangerous. I'll be right down."

On his way to the escalator he hears two short chimes repeated twice alerting the Security people.

Woodforth tells himself to keep it simple. He doesn't know what the man is talking about, but he knows blackmail when he hears it. The man was menacing. Look at him. What could Woodforth do except play along by writing the check?

He feels enormously vindicated.

"Look at us," he demands silently from his podium at the top of the escalator, "Which of us would do this brutish thing?"

In answer he hears the man persist in his cock-and-bull story about tree work, saying he doesn't know what Woodforth is talking about, he had a deal to cut down trees. Woodforth is trying to hang something on him.

It will be in the newspaper that the husband of the deceased said the woodsman tried to blackmail him about seeing him murder his wife, but the woodsman said he didn't know what Woodforth was talking about, the check proved he had been hired to cut wood.

Another wave of weakness washes through Woodforth. He doesn't think he is up to facing people who have read the conflicting stories of the husband of the deceased and the woodsman. He has only to look into his own mind to know which version he would believe.

Nelly Fallower's *Streetcar*

1

YOU had a choice.
    You could go to Upshaw's church where they did a little Brother's Keeper, a little Adultery, Annual Bazaar, Texts (Timothy, Endowment) and Incredible Hymns. Alec and Janice Crevice went there with the other best people.

You could go to St. Litany's where they did Pro-Life, Mass, Church School, Confession, Obedience and Texts (Matthew, Building Fund). The Canestas went there. They kept saying to each other that they had to change—but what would you change to? Everybody else's kids were off-the-wall.

You could join Divine Gossip where (according to who had your ear) they turned over their bank accounts, children, heads and spouses to the management; or they were enviably well-adjusted people who ran the best bakery in town. They did It's All Here and Texts (First Effusions, Revelations). Norris and Cora Brune thought they had made a mistake but they couldn't be sure, perhaps they had not given of themselves enough.

You could go to Beth Shalom (unless they came here this year on Interfaith Day) where they did texts (Judges, Wiesel), Holocaust, Israel and High Holidays. Harvey and Sylvia Zilber went there. They shopped around for a place that did straight ethics but they all did these Incredible Hymns. Anyhow, Harvey was well-known at parties for his song titles ("Haggadah Right to Sing the Blues," "When I Take Meshugga to Tea") and they didn't know how that would fit in.

You could go to Witnesses, First Immersion, Second Coming (breaking ground on Harwich Road, the big foundation in front is the pool), Third Tabernacles (basement of Second National Bank), or Fourth Pentecostal (God's Astrodome at the Rotary) where they preached Chapter and Verse and Just You Wait. Even if you could figure out which was which, nobody went to those churches. So where did they get the money for the gyms and the schools and the station wagons and their own candidate for president? Ernest and Linda Spuhrer went to Fourth Pentecostal and thought: *at last.*

Not to mention (to mention also) Real Baptists, Methodists, Lutherans, Reformeds, Reformed Reformeds, Friends, Scientists, Latter-Day Saints, Congregationalists, Second Immersions, Associateds, Federateds, Uniteds and Amalgamateds, every blessed one of them in this town of Five Thousand Souls (except Beth Shaloms who had to go thirty miles to Hyannis but—according to Benday LaTouche, Realtor, raising his eyebrows—they had an option on the old French Cable Station).

To the astonishment of the MacEavers when they moved down from Pittsburgh, the Presbyterians hadn't made it into the town, hadn't made it even into the telephone directory of any town within twenty miles. Seeing that people they would know went to Upshaw's church, they went there too, even though three centuries ago John MacEver had enrolled in The Glorious Revolution to be rid of that crowd forever.

All this to keep alive, after some two thousand years against forbidding odds, the grudging acceptance of compassion for fellowmen as a worthy emotion in the human breast.

A natural question occurs: How could the world be in such godawful shape with so many good people in it? Look at it another way: How could it be otherwise, with so many—like Arlen and Tina Bestor—still unfolded?

Of significant available affiliations, we have neglected to notice only the New W's where they preached Nicaragua, Poverty (-cure of, not -vow of), Him/Her, Abortion, and texts (Riesman, e. e. cummings). The New W's had branched from the venerable Westham Universalist-Unitarian Church of the

Summer People when they found out they could make a buy on the old Central Skating Rink.

Nelly Fallower would have preferred to worship the deity in his esthetic aspect by joining a play-reading group, leaving His theological aspect to others, but the bay of the old rink had been ingeniously designed with pews that faced as a sanctuary toward the pulpit and reversed to form a theater, the usages curtained from each other, and the latter deployment interested Nelly very much. It provided a new home for The Parish Players. She moved from the old church to the new. Len Fallower went along with what she wanted on these things.

The point of the preceding enumeration is like Thornton Wilder's (here less artfully made—conceded) in assembling his cast on *The Bridge of San Luis Rey*. The names Bestor, Spuhrer, Brune, Zilber, Fallower, MacEaver, Canesta and Crevice—together with Barden Brigham, the new minister at New W—were in some way (cast, props, set, program, costumes, lighting, publicity, ushers) associated with The Parish Players' fall production in Brigham's church; they and a great many more—forty-three names made the program—and the program thanked still others "too numerous to mention who had contributed," a considerable constituency—congregants and prospects—for a minister of a small church in a small town.

"The meaning of ecumenism is not that people get together but what they get together to do," Brigham said, dedicating the new Players curtain and inviting them all to grab a piece of the rope and *pull!*—a symbol. (At another time he said, as was appropriate, that the meaning of ecumenism was not what people did together but that they got together at all.)

The women regarded well the young (thirty, hm? thirty-two?) man with the ascetic profile who might have chosen Hollywood or Broadway but instead had gone the course at Chicago Divinity. His somewhat blond hair fell in the thicknesses of unbraided mooring lines around a head set low on broad shoulders. His voice wandered at ease through lower registers. He had the flat, forward walk of an Indian on the hunt.

Brigham had come to town too late to be encountered at Great Beach with his two young children, but the muscles running down his spine would be twin serpents and his buttock lumpage would be a gymnast's. Quite a minister the New W's had hired themselves. This was his second church. His wife was negligible; concave, child-centered, voluminously skirted, an early marriage.

As it was her turn to direct, Nelly Fallower had the choice of plays and chose *Streetcar*. Followed the usual bitching about Everybody's seen it and Why not something experimental for a change? and Can't we do a musical? of which Nelly disdained to hear a word while she budgeted, cleared the schedule with the house committee, ordered the scripts, and was on the verge of making the cast call when she had a stunning idea.

"What kind of Stanley Kowalski do you think Barden Brigham would make?" she asked Len.

"You're kidding, I hope. A preacher for a part as physical as that?"

"Brigham isn't physical? Do you want to trade genes with me?"

"He's a minister. Stanley is Marlon Brando."

"Which is more plausible—that that pitiful school teacher goes to pieces for an illiterate hunk or for a physical minister?"

"Blanche was ready to go to pieces for anybody. The last five times I saw *Streetcar* she invited in the delivery boy. Stanley shot at the target of opportunity. All I'm saying is that the part isn't written for a minister."

"Wellllll—that's how you read it. Read it with Barden Brigham in mind and see what you think. Would you?"

"What I think is that you have the box office on your mind."

"At my age, good box office for a badly cast play is not interesting. Read it."

Much against her usual Sunday morning principle of worship, which was to rise late, breakfast with the theater pages of two newspapers and whatever magazines were current, and dress at leisure, Nelly decided to go to church to audition the new minister she had heard speak only briefly, at the "Welcome Barden Brigham and Family" dinner.

Len went along to hold the hymnal between them. He could have used the time to sketch houses for the Sea Call Condominium booklet. He was running late on that. Everybody was running late on everything. He used to run late because the beach or golf or a sail or a bag of scallops had to be worked in. Now the Elder Hostel crowd had moved to Cape Cod, and everybody who still had social security deducted ran late to house them, feed them and cut their grass. Even summer churches and little theaters that used to have an off-season had new committees and plays that had to be worked in.

The reversible pews were well-filled, and so many by lively-looking young people in their twenties and thirties. Only a few years ago, in the old church, all the hair in the congregation had been grayer than his. Now there were all those young men and women—often their wives—who ran late in the building trades, kept restaurants, did music, landscaped. Soon they would fill the gap now evident where there should be members in their middle years, and before long they would be identified as the Elder Hostels by the generation now in the classrooms.

As the Fallowers tucked themselves in, Brigham came forward to the pulpit to speak the opening words. Behind his softly-spoken prayer, she detected a volume of voice on call. His arms filled his sleeves. His neck filled his collar. She deduced a figure muscled close to the bone.

He stepped away from the pulpit and stood unobtrusively in the background while four verses of a hymn written for Yma Sumac's range stumbled in broken octaves through the congregation at the organist's donkey pace—*Good God, woman, get moving*. With an actress's quick study, she impatiently picked up the stanza ahead and glanced at the Order of Service for what came next.

The swords-into-ploughshares thing. Today they would be against war. Boredom was not too high a price to pay for the opportunity to audition Brigham, but when they were seated, and the president of the congregation had materialized in their midst with announcements and disappeared again, Brigham came forward from the shadow, entered the pulpit, and launched Isaiah at her—*spears into pruning hooks* in a rising phrase that drove into her throat, and *neither shall they learn war anymore*—each word a blow delivered in his mightiest voice.

"My good God, what a reading!" she muttered.

The next morning Nelly dropped into Brigham's study.

2

He had been aware of her once or twice, and remembered that they were introduced at his welcoming reception. So far as he knew, he had never seen a madam but he supposed that a very successful one looked like this: a full-figured woman, not fat—loose, rather—inside a knitted grass-green dress that avoided holding her too severely accountable for a slothful life. A slightly excessive perfume, and the bash of glinty chestnut hair on a woman of, say, fifty? while no more authentic than purple, which would have been merely funny, challenged him momentarily to experience something larger than life. Then, skin a shade less white than a clown's, and hazel eyes that understood and pardoned.

He couldn't know that she was as reliably chaste as Penelope. Others wove, painted, wrote poetry, picketed; she did theater, and clothed and decorated herself theatrically.

"Good morning. I'm Nelly Fallower, Len Fallower's wife. You don't mind if I call you Barden?"

"I wish you would, Nelly. We've met, you know. Would

you like a cup of coffee?" It was said of the W's that coffee was the first sacrament; sugar, the first schism; cream, the last straw.

"Thank you. Black. By now are you feeling very much at home on the Cape?"

"I don't know where everything is but the people have been wonderful. It's a grand church. Have you been around here long?" Against fading-tan skin his round blue eyes had the steadiness and intensity of ceramic artifacts.

"We washed ashore ten years ago from Connecticut." She didn't want to get into one of those conversations. "I want to talk to you about The Parish Players."

"I'm well aware of them. They are an important part of church life here."

"I'm afraid we get into people's hair sometimes because we monopolize blocks of auditorium time, but I assure you we try to cooperate. Did you ever do any theater?"

"I have to think. Not since high school. I had parts in *The Last Mile* and *The Importance of Being Earnest*." He recited, " 'I fear there can be no possible doubt about the matter. This afternoon during my temporary absence in London on an important question of romance, he obtained admission to my house by means of the false pretense of being my brother—' " They were both laughing.

"Some memory!"

"I don't think I've thought of those lines in fifteen years."

"I came in to ask if you will read for one of the roles in *Streetcar*. After what you just did you can't tell me you have trouble holding lines. Isn't that so?"

He parried. "Then I'd better tell you something else."

"We would love to have you. Do I give you a problem?"

When he didn't reject her out of hand she knew she had him. He said, "I never thought of it. I've seen the play. I really don't have the time."

"I wouldn't worry about that. We're in and out of rehearsals in a night or two *or three for the leads* a week for six weeks *or*

eight for the leads. Then only Friday and Saturday night performances for a month *and a two-week encore if all goes well.*"

"No minister likes to be committed the night before he
preaches."

"I don't want to push you. I can say only that I'm the
director and I want you very much, and you would meet an
awful lot of people you can't meet very easily any other
way."

He was a church-builder. "Have you a part in mind?"

"Not really," she lied. "Among six male roles we'll find
something right for you."

He looked at his calendar. It was the first he had withdrawn
his eyes from hers. Her sense was that Brigham locked onto
what was in front of him with magnetic intensity, and that
she too had been effectively interviewed.

3

"So you got him," Len said. "Does he know what he's reading
for?"

"I let it hang. Now I hope to do better than Jan Crevice for
Blanche. Jan has already talked to me about the part but I
have in mind a Davies woman who lives in Eastham. I don't
think you know her."

"If you don't think so I guess I don't." He relied on her to
tell him whom he knew and whom he didn't in her theater
crowd.

"I heard her read Cathleen in *Riders to the Sea* at the library.
She stuck with me. She isn't any great beauty but she does
look like she would burn briskly in a breeze, and she moves
nicely. I'm going to ask her to read."

"May all your wishes prosper."

"Come to first cast call next Wednesday, would you? I really
would like to know what you think. Have you read it
through?"

"Ask me a question. Do you realize how many months it
takes him to get Blanche to bed?"

"I never gave it a thought. It takes two hours in the theater."

"Seven or eight. Stella is hardly pregnant when Blanche shows up, and he takes her down while Stella is in the hospital. In real life it wouldn't have taken those two a week. No wonder everybody is running late."

They met in a classroom. Len sat behind her, out of the way, so that chairs were open on either side for her Players friends and behind-the-scenes people to drop by. Nelly talked to them and to the readers, and as the play provided only Blanche with set speeches, Nelly kept on pairing readers in order to hear them in enough dialogue. After Barden Brigham read a passage of Mitch with Ethel Davies reading Stella, Nelly said,

"While you're here, Barden, please leaf over to page forty and read Stanley's lines. Mrs Davies—Ethel—would you pick up Blanche, beginning 'The poor little thing was out there listening to us' thank you?"

She watched how they might work together.

"Keep going. Ethel, it's coming out a little coy. Can you give us a little more bitchiness? If the character is too coy Stanley gets a bellyful and wants her soon gone. The name of the play is *Desire*. Take it, please?"

Nelly got up and turned her back on the dialogue in order to hear it better. She kept an eye on Len for a signal.

"Yes," she said next day to Brigham in his study, "it surprised me too. I was thinking Mitch for you. I didn't doubt that you could do Stanley but I thought that without any recent theater work, you might not be ready. You're such a quick study, though—"

After the second cast call Janice Crevice waited until Nelly dismissed and sat down beside her. She took Nelly's hand to create a bond. "Listen, Nelly, I want a real crack at Blanche before you lock it up. You owe me a full chance. I turn out for every production and I take whatever the part is. I would like to read against anybody"—she didn't say, "Who the hell is this Davies?"—"on the Belle Reve speech and the cemetery

speech and any of the dialogues with Stanley and Stella. I
want to feel I have a real shot, Nelly."

"Why would you think I want you to have anything less?
We've done a lot of plays together, Jan. The part certainly
isn't locked in my mind. You're right there."

"I had a feeling. I want you to know how I feel. This play is
made to order for you, and that Brigham man is either a
disaster or genius-casting for Kowalski. This *Streetcar* is going
to be a real fireball. I would just love to do Blanche. You don't
think I'm too old?"

"It's written for a thirty-five-year-old woman."

"A beat-up thirty-five, Nelly. I could make that weight."

"You're a stately beauty, Jan. I'm trying to see you fragile
enough."

"Believe me, I'm fragile."

4

"All right, we'll quit here. Thank you all. I'd like everybody
back in two weeks — Tuesday — not line-perfect but reading
meaningfully, please? We'll begin reading through. Stanley
and Blanche, could we get together to establish characters for
a couple of hours before that? Next week? Tuesday? Not to
forget Stella. Stella should come in for that session. Is that all
right, Linda? Linda Spuhrer, do you hear me? Can you make
it? Good. Barden, Ethel and Linda next Tuesday here at
seven? Thanks all."

She told Len how it worked out.

"So you wound up with new Players in both leads."

"Three leads. Stella too. This is the Spuhrer girl's first play
anywhere."

"It's a Guinness. The regulars must be ready to shoot you."

"Janice Crevice is pissed not to get Blanche, but Davies is so
right."

"They'll never let you do another play."

"Open casting is open casting. Give me a light one while
you're mixing."

He brought it to her. Before he handed it over he bent to kiss her. She winked and offered her mouth on a silver platter. They had been through the wars. Money struggle and sexual doubt were behind them, old boyfriends now surely only old friends, pretty girls merely ornaments, some countries—even continents—no longer necessary to visit.

"We're going to have a play," she said after they let go. "What have you been doing?"

"More sketches and the Sox."

"How did we do?"

"We win easy. Six-two. Clemens all the way."

Alone by himself all evening, sketching, and watching a ball game, and still he was bow-tied and jacketed, and his shirt-cuff reached elegantly from his sleeve as he pushed his glasses higher on the bridge of his nose. His sly smile foretold that he was thinking of something she might find amusing.

"I've been thinking about your play. Do you think Williams may have mixed up the sisters?"

"I'm not with you."

"Stella's the one that's sexed-up, not Blanche. This Blanche is full of problems—money, alcohol, image. Sex is the least. But that's all there is to Stella. Stella wasn't drunk or broke or over-the-hill when she left the old plantation. She took off with this grunt, married him, lives in a shack with him, and he hasn't a thing in the world going for him except organ music."

"That's something, darling. Be fair. He also fixes some kind of machinery."

"Hers. That's what I've been telling you."

"Well we're not playing it that way, darling. We're playing it the way Tennessee wrote it. Stella is 'a gentle woman . . . of a background obviously quite different from her husband's.' "

"I'm just telling you how it is in the real world."

They were all the way to the fruit cup before the telling point she had been mulling clarified for her. "Count Vronsky didn't have anything going for him either. All he did was ride horses and run around with the boys. Anna threw herself under a train for him."

"So we are told. Anything goes in a costume piece."

"Are only men allowed to blow their lives in the real world?"

He didn't want to be trapped on the wrong side of a women's-lib argument. A few years ago he might have said Yes as more or less of a joke, but his playing field had been narrowed. "Oh no, but a man who has money problems, alcohol problems and image problems—would you say he is a sex maniac if he depends on the kindness of strange girls? The real question is, which of the *sisters* was sexed-up?"

"You're simplifying. It isn't what I say, it's what Tennessee Williams says."

"He might have been the last to know."

"You can do the next *Streetcar*. Would you believe that a pretty girl like Spuhrer comes from one of those fun churches? The Immersions or something?"

5

Rehearsals went well. She cut Stanley's line "I never was a very good English student" because Williams hadn't written any speeches that made that necessarily so. She looked at pronouns and verb tenses Williams had embedded like raisins in a loaf to authenticate the working-class origins of the hunk, let some of them stand, changed a few. The character was a troubleshooting engineer who got around; as Stella said, a cut above his pals.

Nelly led Brigham to read the part more for nature than neighborhood; he was good at lowering the level of his class accents. He had to monkey with his voice anyhow to get the New Orleans into it. The terse, rude reading confirmed the animality of Brigham when he stripped to his skiv for the last rehearsals.

Ethel Davies lacked beauty and used no makeup—she could have been cast as a governess—but neither had she liabilities. She had voice, and the unhurried confidence of women with well-made bodies that in time they will prevail; the script and the author's insistence that Blanche be vulnerable and fearful and speak in nervous bursts remained accountable to that remote source of her authority.

As the *Streetcar* company became increasingly accustomed to itself, a subterranean curiosity grew about what might be going on or come to be going on between the minister and the female lead.

If they sat aside to read together, if he brought her a Coke or she lighted his cigarette, if they were up in their lines and laughed, or arrived together, or walked side-by-side across the dark parking lot to their cars, the thought occurred: something's in the air. It was disappointing that the way the part was written the two of them never embraced. It wasn't until very late in the evening that she fell to the floor and he picked her up and carried her to the bed. He never kissed her. Disappointing.

Nelly didn't think anything would go on.

She had been through it many times. A theater company was a denser saturation of personal relationships than any other brief encounter between strangers. The premise of being actors at all was an ability and a desire to release the ordinary restraints of voice and personality into the custody of third parties free to act the logic of parts; and as there would be no audience for parts that asked actors to act less strangely or freely than they did on the street, writers did not write them. Acting, therefore, was in Nelly Fallower's understanding the practice of uncommon liberties by people made uncommonly attractive, interesting, well-spoken, sympathetic, bold and so on by parts.

An amateur could be suspected of lingering in a part when he left the stage, but a professional was practiced in letting go. Brigham had a credential even more convincing than his credential as an actor to rely on: he was a minister.

"Ministers don't have to join theater groups to have affairs.

They know the rules. They don't break down for every chick that goes by."

"Not every," he said.

"They are both married and have children. They are adults. I don't know about her, but I count on him absolutely. Nothing is going to go on."

Nelly didn't want anything to go on.

"If anything happens it better be late in the run. We're really in good shape and I don't want trouble."

Nelly was ready to put it all together.

"Please, no books tonight. You should be speech-perfect. Jan Crevice has the prompt book but I would like to see you push through without help. Scenes One through Four. You are on the set. You are real people. All of you are living real lives. Two women are fighting for this man. Rough gestures will be rough. Kisses will be kisses. I would prefer not to break. Go right through. I'll call any stops. Enter Stanley and Mitch. Let's go?"

Barden was into Kowalski's skin. He was Stanley Kowalski who had graduated from high school, had a good blue-collar job, and still liked to run with the guys. Perhaps he had not fulfilled his early promise and was more comfortable bullying inferiors. The business Nelly had invented for him, the shoulder spasm which threw off every constraint, worked well. They all were doing well. Especially gratifying was seeing Linda Spuhrer keep the pace.

Occasionally Nelly said a word for the director's script to Sylvia Zilber on her left—"Slower here . . . Mitch moving too much . . ." and even less often did Janice Crevice on her other hand have to call a cue. Very well indeed, through Scene One and Scene Two, into Scene Three, and now the powerful passage where the pregnant Stella who has run away to the upstairs neighbors is summoned back by an anguished Stanley in his Isaiah voice—"with heaven-splitting violence" as the author commanded—

"STELL-LAHHHH!"

The upstairs door opens. Stella comes down the rickety

stairs. They stare at each other, reconciling their difference through desire. Her eyes glisten with tears. They embrace passionately. Nelly thinks it is too sidelong, a tango. The author did not contemplate that they will stand there moaning passionately with estranged bodies.

"Wait, wait! You are husband and wife. You are lovers. Dig into each other. Again down the last few steps, Stella please?"

They do a little better, working freer of their self-consciousness, but not as real as it is going to be for a *Streetcar* directed by Nelly Fallower. She hates to break but she must. "Better, but let's have it again from the top of the stairs, please? This time remember who you are. You are Stella and Stanley. You made a baby together."

From the top of the stairs. The tears. The coming together, the moans—yes, that's it—and Stanley dropping to his knees, to kiss his child in her belly. Stella takes his head and raises it to her level—marvelous, how she sways!—and he picks her up—he will snatch open the screen door and take her into the house toward the necessary bed, the destination Blanche will not reach until six scenes later—but now what?

Brigham holds her as if he does not know what to do with her. She should be clinging to him, her knees bent in a position of arousal but she is limp, sagged against him, and he not only has to carry her, he has to carry her dead weight. He calls, "Would anybody have smelling salts? I'm afraid she's out. It does seem hot in here."

He eases her down on the step while Nelly and others come toward them rapidly. Nelly looks for something to elevate the girl's legs. "Give me those chair cushions?" Someone thinks somebody should call the Rescue Squad.

"Wait, people, wait," Ed Canesta begs. "Give her a minute. It may be nothing." Kids don't get heart attacks. Kids don't die just like that. It could be heat, in heat, period, stress.

No smelling salts can be found in the first-aid box; Cora Brune goes to the cleaning closet for ammonia. Tina Bestor brings a glass of water. Nelly asks for a wet cold cloth, and before it arrives Linda's eyes open to a dozen faces hovering over her. Nelly asks, "Are you all right, Linda?"

The girl's face wavers in distress. She turns on her side and draws up her knees. My God, she's praying! "Dear Jesus Christ forgive me for I have sinned. Dear Jesus Christ forgive me for I have sinned. Dear Jesus Christ—"

"No no, Linda," Brigham says and sits beside her. He puts his hand on her shoulder. "You're a good person." She pulls away and says, "Don't touch me. You are evil. Lord Jesus Christ forgive us."

Nelly has heard enough. She gestures for Brigham to make way for her and takes his place beside the girl. He walks away from the group and turns his back to the set. Nelly says, "You'll be all right, Linda. Rest here for a few minutes. Somebody will take you home. Are you driving?"

Linda shakes her head. Her husband will be there for her at ten-thirty.

Nelly decides to take her home herself. They may be able to talk. She tells the cast to go on without her. Jan will read Stella. Wednesday night same time, beginning with Scene Four.

6

Nelly believed that the human voice, pitched properly, could solve any problem short of a notorious disease. She drove slowly to delay arriving at the nearby address while she tried the worldly, the complicitory, the chummy, the authoritative. The girl sobbed, shuddered and remained silent or uttered incantatory nonsense about evil and sin.

The sympathy Nelly assumed she had for any human being—or dog for that matter—in distress, no matter how self-inflicted or mindless the origin, evaporated. The girl might ruin her play! Arrived at the house, she laid an arm across Spuhrer's lap and wouldn't let her escape.

"Now talk to me, Linda. You owe it to me. You owe it to all

of us. You owe it to yourself to come to terms with this. What can I do to help you?"

"You can't save me from sin." She put it as an accusation.

"Oh sin." How could she go about telling the girl she could have Brigham wear a jockstrap. An athletic supporter. A chastity belt. She must know it under some name. "I'm sure Barden doesn't think he is engaged in sin with you. He is in the part."

"I shouldn't have tried out. My mother was right. My husband and my father were right. I was willful."

Willful, yes, that was what will was for, to be used against opposition. "But you did try out. You have the part and you are very good in it. Everybody loves you as Stella."

Linda put her hands on Nelly's arm firmly, to tell her she wanted to be released. "Please let me go now. I wanted to be somebody in my house. I wanted to do something they would notice. I was wrong to do this."

"But why? What is so terrible? Why would you leave people in the lurch when they rely on you?"

"The Lord Jesus Christ relied on me and I failed Him."

"Oh now, Linda. You didn't fail anybody. We are made in God's image. He must have certain expectations." She realized that she was unable to handle God in His theological aspect and had nothing convincing to say. The only text she could think of was that one about swords and ploughshares. "Get a good night's sleep. Beat your swords into ploughshares and we can talk tomorrow."

Tomorrow Linda spoke through her mother. "She can't, do you understand? She can't."

Nelly was livid. What kind of religion was this? What kind of God did she worship that told her to walk out two weeks before the opening? Didn't she read the play? Didn't she know what the play was about? Didn't she know what life was about? She asked the questions of her husband, who was not able to supply satisfactory answers.

She talked to Barden Brigham. "I want you to know that

everybody thinks you are giving a marvelous, human, real performance. The cast is behind you one hundred percent."

"I appreciate it. We should all think first of finding a way to reach out to Linda. She won't talk to me on the phone. I am very much concerned about you too, about your play. What are you going to do?"

"We're going to open."

"Who will do Stella?"

"A grown woman."

She had expected to find Brigham down. He was serious, which was not the same thing. She perceived that Brigham faced into the situation as a walker faces into bad weather and finds it, if not agreeable, at least stimulating, which is a kind of agreeability. Barden Brigham didn't really mind bad weather. Nelly's mind leaped: she thought there must be more to Mrs Brigham than met the eye, or else the woman was in for a hard time.

Nelly was wokking up dinner when Len came home, washed, poured a drink and sat down in the living room to look at the Boston paper. Their conversation volleyed between the two rooms. She brought him up-to-date on Spuhrer's decision, on her conversation with Brigham, on the search she had begun to find somebody who had played a decent Stella in another production.

"Do you remember the girl who did Stella in Harwich a couple of years ago?"

"I don't remember. Don't you have an understudy?"

"Come in here and talk to me. I can't hear half what you're saying."

He carried his drink into the efficient small rectangle that was their kitchen. "I asked you if you had an understudy for Stella."

"Yes, of course, I have Lou MacEaver but she's weak."

He saw the lettuce, the carrot, the green pepper, the tomato, the salad bowl. He could be useful. He began to strip the carrot.

"What about Janice Crevice? She must have the part down."

"Len, you aren't serious. Crevice is too old to do Big Sistah, so how can she do Stella?"

"Williams wrote the play upside-down. The older sister would have been the first to leave good old Belle Reve, and she was the sexed-up one. Jan can play that."

"Come on, Len."

"She can. Make Brigham a few years older."

"Don't be ridiculous. The script says she's Blanche's younger sister. She behaves like a younger."

"You can change a few words of script. You already changed it for Brigham."

"I don't think this is one of your better ideas."

"You win some and you lose some. Is it too soon to put in the oil and vinegar?"

7

"Listen, you two," Nelly said, "this play is in your hands. What do you think? Can you do it?"

"Barden and I can do it all right," Jan said. "We'll have to put something into makeup. Barden, can you age?"

"I'm not getting any younger doing this play."

Nelly used the disaster to demand more time that nobody would refuse. She had something going every night—sections of dialogue, scenes and more scenes and curtain-to-curtain. The poker players became professional. Mitch came to know what it was to be enwrapped by this fancy woman, not just say the playwright's lines. Stella and Blanche became sisters. Barden of all people could not refuse her time. Stanley and Blanche got their menacing timing down. Stanley and Stella became lovers who could be interrupted but not destroyed.

On their fourth day together—the tenth or twelfth time they attacked the scene at the bottom of the stairs—as he scraped down the length of her body to kiss her belly, Jan Crevice sank her head to his and whispered, "It's okay, honey, okay, okay. I'm with you all the way."

"Those two read the script," Len told Nelly. He opened her book to the playwright's instructions and ran his finger under the line . . . *they come together with low animal moans.* "You think Tennessee Williams doesn't know the English language well enough to say what he wants?"

Word went around that *Streetcar* was in trouble, and that it would be just as well to wait until the third or fourth week for tickets, give the play a chance to settle down. Nelly wanted another week—every director wants another week—but after the first dress rehearsal she didn't feel that she *needed* it.

"We have a good production. I don't need anybody to tell me if the production is good or not," she said, which was true but not entirely.

The definition of a good play for The Parish Players had to be spoken at the box office, for there were no endowments, no grants. Program advertising—mentioning the forty-three names and others "too numerous to mention" engaged in the production—reflected amounts too insignificant for merchants to decline, and memberships were merely tickets pre-sold at a discount. Despite her bravura assertion that her judgment was accountable to nobody, Nelly very much wanted to hear from the opening night that the audience was going out in a mood to sell tickets word-of-mouth.

The closing ovation was heavy and sustained, surging when she thought they were about ready to let it go. The audience got to its feet and roared, "Hooray," "Bravo," "Bravissimo" and "Bene Bene." Friends exchanged victory signs and winks of approval as they inched toward the doors. The house had the unmistakable look of a good night at the theater.

Len said, "They didn't have that 'Let's get out of here, get the car and go home' look."

The review in the *Fog* assured a sellout—and a two-week encore Brigham hadn't been warned about.

Nelly Fallower turned the fall production of The Parish Play-
ers into a director's tour de force with her reading of A Streetcar Named Desire, *the Tennessee Williams play that opened*
Friday in the Parish Hall of the New Unitarian-Universalist
church in South Westham. Even if you've seen ten Streetcars,
get tickets for the eleventh . . .

8

That summer, Barden and Jan found that they could no
longer stand it; that their children were better off abandoned
than to grow up in loveless homes; that one lived only one
sacred life and had a duty to hold onto love with all despera-
tion once it was found; that people must be talking, and it
was dishonorable to expose their spouses to scandal; and that
they would declare themselves and take off.

They had four splendid years together in a Rhode Island
town where Brigham obtained a parish. The Bestors had
friends there who told them that Brigham filled the pews of a
failing church so full that they were talking about double
services and building on. It was too bad, but it was said that
Brigham and Jan were not getting along. You know how
people talk, there were rumors that he was involved with
another woman.

The next play Nelly asked for was *Othello*.

"Really?" Len asked, poking his glasses up to the bridge of
his nose. "Are you going to do it for what it is?"

"What is that?"

"A play about homosexuality."

"I never heard of that," she said doubtfully.

"Othello and Iago. Desdemona was meant to be a cover but
her role changed. She came between them. Think about it."

"But Shakespeare didn't write it that way."

"Oh well, Nelly. Shakespeare. Deconstruct him. Writers
are always the last to know."

Gibson #7

HE cleansed himself of luxury in a shack on Cape Cod, dozing in the sun, belly down, furry, cooked like an end cut; in minimum trunks, a towel over the sensitive skin of the stump, a mañana hat protecting his neck and bald spot. He did not identify the voices. He faked sleep while he thought, who? They asked for his attention with dribbles of sand which he shook off for green flies that had overstayed the notice given by the first full August moon. He heard softly said, "Uncle Lloyd. Uncle Lloyd."

Breaking into the sun, he might not have known them immediately without "Uncle"; shaded by cowboy hats, behind sulphur lenses and grannies, clothes piled on their hips like carried laundry, only tank-shirts intervening between them and the world. Maxine's twins. With them were a Cro-Magnon man and Thomas Jefferson (maybe Robespierre, the all-purpose jagged profile; the peruke).

"Jill! Barbara! It's absolutely great of you to come by!"

"Mother said if we got to the Cape we had to look you up."

"Do you have to be ordered? How is your mother? I missed her the last time she was in New York. Aunt Lois saw her."

"She's fine. This is Harvey. This is Michael."

They had driven down from Maine. They were selling pots. It could be worse. It could be singular.

He and Maxine talked every couple of weeks so he kept up.

Maxine had nearly collapsed when the twins told her they were dropping out. On school holidays and in phone calls they leaked intimations, but she thought she could jolly them along, it couldn't happen to her kids, they had too much sense. Supporting civil rights was one thing. She expected that of her children. Negroes — (*Blacks, all right, blacks, whatever.* She learned to say "black" early, it was what they wanted, although she thought it sounded just as strange to most of them as it did to her, it was no big deal. She learned to capitalize it; it was up to them.) Blacks were Americans, it was outrageous that they couldn't go into the same schools and restaurants and use a bathroom in a gas station like everybody else. If Jill and Barbara wanted to take a stand on that, fine, God bless them.

"Write to the school paper. Go to meetings. Write to your senator. That's more than nine-tenths of everybody you know will ever do. That's more than I do. Take up social work."

"All that does is make it look as if something is going on. What's going on is that it gets worse every day."

"That's not true. I'm not shilling for the way things are, but the condition of black people can't be compared to what it was a generation ago. What they call poverty today and what it was when you were born can't be compared. In your own lifetime the medical progress —"

"Mother —" with patience, Maxine had always done her best for them, but the system was built into her — "that has nothing to do with it. It wouldn't hurt if everybody died a year or two sooner if we all lived with love and compassion."

"There is no such thing as 'we all.' Any time you read we all have to do this or that before anything happens, just turn the page. There is just this person and that person."

"Yeah well. Living forever isn't everything."

"See how you feel about that when you're your grandmothers' age."

"A few rich people get double bypasses and the president is in a whole new fucking war in Vietnam. The garbage man picks up *your* garbage twice a week —"

That's an offense?

"Other people *live* in garbage. The whole system has to be turned around."

"It won't happen."

"You just can't say it won't happen. It has to happen."

"A lot of things that have to happen don't happen."

Ease off, tempers were rising. Confrontation would get nowhere. The object was to talk them back to school for another term. "Don't give away your own life to save a world that may not appreciate it. Go back to school for another lousy eight or nine months and you'll have a degree. If you ever want to teach you'll have the degree."

"Who wants to teach? The Black Death."

"When you have children and they leave the nest you'll thank your stars for your degrees. Stay in school. Transfer to something nearer the action if you want. New School or something. Finish this last one lousy year. What does it amount to?"

They refused to be swept into the pan. At least they had come home to tell her, they hadn't sent a card from San Francisco.

"Okay, then. Take a semester off. Go to Europe. See the great sights. See the galleries. You may be right, it could be better than school. Then come back and finish up. You wouldn't have to finish at Wells. You could do your senior year at the New School or the University of Hawaii. Arizona. Black Mountain." *What the hell was Black Mountain?* She had read it somewhere. Every last word she had ever read seemed to be secreted in her pores, waiting to sweat.

They already were thinking about Europe. But no grand tour. Hitchhike from Paris to Athens.

"Oh come on. Do you know what can happen to girls hitchhiking in Europe? Stand on a street corner in Italy sometime before you decide to hitchhike across Europe. Will you please do me a favor and talk to your uncle Lloyd?"

He didn't have children. He wouldn't understand.

"Will you please do me a favor and call him?"

He told them he didn't think it was a very good idea. By then they were going to go with two boys. Maxine hadn't heard about boys—

"What boys? Not that—that—?"

Different boys.

"Okay, you always had good judgment. I could always trust you when you were little so I have to trust you now. Let's talk about taking care of yourself. You have dams, use them. Don't do anything you'll regret." *Jesus H. Christ, do you know how dumb this all sounds?* "Come upstairs with me for one minute. I want to show you something."

She marched them to the bedroom that had been theirs since they were six. Banners and crayon-paintings, photos of radio singers, album posters, Howdy Doody, photos of the gang, moth-eaten animals. *Their* attachments, not hers. Two worn and glossy maple beds.

"These are your beds. There isn't anything you can do to make them not yours as long as you live. Is that straight? As long as you live, this is the place you can come home to. Don't forget I'm your mother." (She asked Lloyd, *What do you live for except to see that your own flesh and blood don't fall into holes too deep to get out of?*) "Don't fill your heads with any goddamn drugs."

They sat beside her and told her not to worry. Barbara didn't know whether she owed it to Maxine to tell her or owed it to her to not tell her she was pregnant and was going to get an abortion next week. She told her.

Stupefying. "Not by some goddamn voodoo?"

Somebody reliable in Brooklyn.

"How can there be anybody reliable in Brooklyn?" Brooklyn was another *Butterfield 8*. They wouldn't know *Butterfield 8*. All they knew was *today*. All they read was *today*.

She heard herself in flip-voice and pulled back. "I give you credit not to be such a goddamn fool as to risk anything like this with a goddamn voodoo. This is a serious thing, you know. Let me find you a real doctor."

"This is a real doctor, he really cares."

"Caring is one thing. He has a knife. You're going to be in a room with a man who has a knife. What do you know about him?"

They knew somebody who knew.

They didn't know anything. "When is it supposed to happen?"

"Tuesday morning."

"I'll be there."

"That isn't necessary. I have Jill."

"Jill is not your mother. Where was Jill when you got a pregnancy you don't want? I'll be there." She wanted to look at the doctor. They wouldn't know how to make a scene and get out of there if he was a voodoo. She knew how to make a scene.

She looked the doctor in the eye. She looked around his office. He seemed to be all right. How did you ever really find out anything about doctors? He seemed to care. He was all right.

A month after Tuesday they went to Europe; and back to Washington, Denver, Chicago, San Francisco. Maxine kept him current. Maxine was verbal. She should have been an academic. Now for the first time he knew more than she did about her daughters: they were traveling with a Cro-Magnon man and Robespierre and selling pottery.

And how were the pots going?

Everybody thought the pots were *great*. They began in Sandwich and worked their way down the north shore and had lots of orders. They were going back by the south shore.

He and Lois began coming to Truro in 1949 and stayed some time every summer since, always at the Gibson cottages, a string of ramshackle one-room unpainted dustbowl shacks teetering on the Truro dune. The cottages were unnamed, just plain-Jane numbers. Gibson #7 was no worse or better than the others, except that it had a porch, the kind gaunt men in flannel shirts and suspenders sat on, smoking pipes with taped stems in Walker Evans photographs.

When casino-time passed after the first World War the derelict in the valley was sawed apart, recarpentered into cottages and impaled on the dune; twelve slow-dying subvertebrates against which cruelty was allowed, gapping and curling in the wind-blast and parch of the sun. Electricity sagged from shack to shack, dropping sixty-watt bulbs from frayed wires, one to a living room, one to a bedroom. The bedroom was a third of the living room partitioned off. Lloyd detected symbolism in the uncovered studs on the sleeping side.

Every year when she first looked in the bedroom Lois shook her head and said, "Really, Lloyd—" or "I'd forgotten—"

The bed was stuffed into a corner in order to make an aisle on the opposite side to stand in. A woman with a strong back came from the village every morning with the mail and the grocery order from yesterday, made the bed, did the kitchen and bathroom and generally brushed the place up. Instead of a telephone, Mrs Hooter scuffed over from the manager's cottage with messages. She was obliging, but tenants told people to think twice before calling. If they wanted calls they would be someplace else.

Gibson cottages were hard to get and Truro had no better address. Mingled with admiration for the Perlemans' stamina to survive here was envy of their success in getting a lease. That the rent was insignificant made it all the more certain that they had not bribed their way in but were there solely because Mrs Hooter said so, according to what standard Lloyd never found out.

Apart from the cachet, the attractions were the accessibility of the ocean at the foot of the dune and the view. The full moon in clouds over the ocean was an incomparable display, longer-lasting and more conducive to contemplation than the sunsets that were the pride of the other side. On its way to those glorious sets the sun made the bay houses uninhabitable on their view side after three o'clock.

On rainy days the Hooter people forsook their dune and dropped in on Al, Henry, Bunny, Naomi, Hannah, Zolly or Victor in the lowlands where they drank too much, spoke with unnecessary candor and realized intensely that death was a day nearer every day and the only cure was divorce.

Not that Mrs. Hooter's tenants were alone in these derelictions, it was only that sixty watts were so few when first light was two hours late and the forecast was no let-up in the all-day rain. On such days the shallow porch was a privilege of rank, unless the weather came off the water or the greenflies were still around; then even the Perlemans left the dune.

Early in their careers they took a Gibson for a week, then for two, then a month. Now the cottage had accumulated some of their permanent things—a refrigerator, a quick-oven, a bed, a sofa and reading chair—and they kept it for the season. Lois never stayed more than a week, seldom as much, and Lloyd usually gave up after two or three. A friend had a standing offer to use it anytime in the off-weeks. He and his family tried it once. His wife thereafter booked them to mountains or deserts or to worse beaches in farther places with inns that advertised.

Lois wished the cottage were not only hard to get but impossible. If they had to come to Truro, to which she was by no means committed, she would rather make do with something less austere on Pamet. She didn't make a fuss about it because after a few dutiful days she went off to visit her brothers and sisters or get some of her own work done without interruption. Her husband was well-settled. He was not difficult about food. For breakfast: cereal or a piece of pastry and coffee. For lunch: a sandwich and a piece of fruit. After four years Mrs Hooter allowed them to bring in a real refrigerator with a freezer shelf. If Lloyd didn't accept a dinner invitation or meet somebody at a restaurant he defrosted a casserole and bluffed up a salad.

The reasons for his attachment to this dreary place were complex. He advertised that his tastes were simple and he needed nothing more than to lie in the sun and read, but that did not require a place so spectacularly primitive as Gibson #7. It would not have been difficult to build something sufficiently modest in Truro that would still have reliable plumbing and a place to plug in a hundred-watt lamp. Lois suggested it. They discussed it. He didn't do it. Human beings often have peculiar purposes, and arrive at their ends by extremely devious routes. Lois had no reason to think particularly of Ada Downse or Justinia. She knew him to be reliable.

"Could we use the bathroom, Uncle Lloyd? How about showers?"

The bathroom was inside, not altogether a certainty in the architecture. Having ascertained the location, a visitor who was not terminally obliged to it might look the facilities over and decide, what's the rush? He heard flushings plumb the well, and the groaning slave of a pump draw valuable rusted water. Sand would be in the water tomorrow. Glass was made of sand. It could make the gut hemmorhage. Put bottled water on the grocery order.

"Could we set up our sleeping bags out here?"

"It's against the rules, but we won't bring that up. Wait until after dark."

Nobody else dropped in expecting to camp without notice. It was known that he lived ascetically at Truro. Maxine knew even she would be lodged in a motel. Why visit and stay in a motel? He was visited at Princeton. Maxine's twins were their own law.

He was not even sure that he had any emotion for them more intense than relationship. For Maxine, yes. She survived wonderfully after losing Dan. She had the family brains and wit. He had offered her a job on the magazine but she wanted to go on with that advertising work that didn't challenge her at all, and she did well. But her twins—after Dan was killed in the Pacific it fell to Lloyd to stand to them more or less as father. He did not know what do with the role when it was more than transient and convivial and involved parental responsibility.

They were really not attractive and did nothing to mitigate the deficiency. Their skin was a desert. They hadn't learned to speak properly. They might as well have been raised in a garage. They had no profession. They believed in nothing real, especially not bras, and driveled about better worlds and mantras and peace and love.

Maxine had reported a conversation. "It wouldn't make any difference if we lived a year or two less if we lived with compassion and love." They had no idea what they meant by love. They had no idea what they meant by anything.

They said "love" as if it were a commodity like potatoes. You were supposed to love Indians. You were supposed to love everybody on the block. You were supposed to love plants. Whales. The human race hadn't even made it to loving enemies as thyself and it was supposed to love whales.

He did not regret having given the African bishop a hard time about love last month. They had got on the better for it. It had been good for Twana—a really first-class man—for a change not to talk to somebody who nodded his head solemnly to hear, "We need your gift of love . . ."

"Love is such a useful word, sir . . ." It gave Lloyd satisfaction to call strangers "sir" in his unservile voice; it dignified them both but, oddly, more himself, in the saying. "The modern thrust of language is toward specific meaning. Do you mind if I as a married man am unable in all honesty to consider a gift of love? Would a check be acceptable?"

He wouldn't have said it if he hadn't seen in the black Right Reverend Sir's brilliantly intelligent eyes that he was capable of banter. A Banterstan. Bishop Twana's mouth flexed constantly, licked at by his tongue as if foraging the environment for nuances that did not come adequately through other senses. The hands that he clapped vigorously to his arms, embracing Lloyd's wit, were like Lloyd's the hands of a laborer. A remarkable man. The clergyman's eyes widened in appreciation as Lloyd went on, "For you, sir, as an individual, on this short acquaintance I already feel a great affection. The language affords me a way to express it without compromising the meaning the word 'love' has—"

Twana's face erupted in laughter, as if he had never heard quite such a good joke. His mouth disclosed a course of trophy teeth as white as his collar. Against his better judgment, knowing the joke had not been quite that good, Lloyd found himself feeling a discipleship to a man who appreciated him so thoroughly. Not love, but it was understandable that the man was loved. That is to say, admired. Worshipped, perhaps; Twana wouldn't especially like being worshipped. Respected. Regarded affectionately.

"The check, yes, the check," Twana laughed, taking out a huge handkerchief to deal with his tears; and then was suddenly sober. In the white drama of the handkerchief and the teeth and the collar and the frosting on his tightly fitted cap of hair, the clergyman's face was illuminated by a manifestation of such ardent kindness that Lloyd thought himself in the presence of the *shining from shook foil* of Hopkins's celestial vision.

To speak of love one surely had to speak of shook foil; desire such as had shown forth when he and Lois first looked deeply at each other, not merely sentiment or intellectual disposition. Otherwise, what distinct meaning did it have?

Still (*how the man's eyes showed forth!*) love as desire had been more an announcement that something more complex was in the vicinity than it was the thing itself. And the thing itself was quite different for others than it had been for him. For Gide's Immoralist love first made itself known as pity, a quality that never entered the transaction with Lois. The Immoralist loved a condition; an orphan, a pitiable condition, at once individual and universal. If they wanted a universal emotion, then, why didn't they call it pity and leave love out of it?

Pity was certainly a large state to aspire to. Nobody had ever moved the world an inch by loving it; but many by pity. Unlike love, of which not a trace remained if it spilled into the reservoir of humanity, pity was as efficacious for misfortune in Africa as in the neighborhood, and had got Gide's man a wife. The only limitation was that one didn't pity trees. Living creatures, yes; whales, yes; caterpillars, less so. Trees, no; although Cleve Baxter had those nutty experiments going with plants . . .

Twana would suppose that the notation Perleman made in

the small spiral-bound notebook on his desk was to fix something about the conversation for reference—and it did. *Twana Love Pity Gide Jesus. Fl Nightingale. Cleve Baxter says plants (love?) human beings.* The memo might jog a thousand words for his page.

Twana said, "But I know if my people had your love, the check would be greater."

"Would you take the love without the check?"

Twana appeared to give it profoundly serious consideration. "Yes," he said. "If my people had Lloyd Perleman's love, I would take it instead of a check."

"Today," Lloyd said in irony.

"The checks would come in time, and they would be greater. They would give you greater happiness to sign, Mr. Perleman."

Lloyd signed a larger check than he had had in mind and told Twana something he would ordinarily have thought imprudent. "We will not forget you, Bishop. You can come back."

"We love you, Mr Perleman, if you do not yet love us."

Even with that deft interjection *yet* all that about love had to be consummate nonsense; but the man was a great artist, and his life—his very life—was offered in the performance. For what he insisted on being, the life-enjoying Right Reverend Sir could be a dead man tomorrow morning. No man of the West—maybe a dissident Russian or a Flying Wallenda strolling the unaproned wire—but none of Lloyd's friends fiddling and pecking and painting or preaching in what Saul called the Central Command Post of Comprehension—could say anything like that.

"Whom else do you expect to call on while you're over here?"

Twana challenged him. "Anyone you are kind enough to refer me to."

That Maxine cared greatly for her daughters Lloyd didn't doubt—but was that love? Probably for her. If it meant their lives, Maxine was a good bet to get out on that high wire and make a run for it. But for all their talk about love, would they do it for her? Ah, but now he was reflecting not about love but about death. He regretted that the natural direction of any active mind was astray.

To be fair, one thing was in the twins' favor: they were not partial to creature comforts. He liked them having visual proof of how little he needed. It took the curse off the great house in Princeton they knew him by. The refrigerator and the quick-oven spoke for the outlet on the wall. Two lamps no secondhand store would have the gall to put a price on spoke for the kickboard.

"On a cold damp day I have to disconnect a lamp in order to plug in a heater. I suppose Lincoln would have found that luxurious, though." The smiles were vague. The boys might not know who Lincoln was. "You know Lincoln? A member of the establishment of his time." Being a man of letters in this humble place, he surely was not regarded as entirely of the establishment. The girls surely knew he opposed the war.

To his inquiry they said they would like to eat Italian. He took them to a table-jammed low-ceilinged room. The crowd was touristy, he didn't know anybody in the room but Cuzo and Kelly, although some undoubtedly knew him. He made a point of speaking of Vietnam—"*the fuckin' war*"—, killing two birds with one stone. He excused himself to make a phone call. He told Ada not tonight. He had unforeseen guests. Family.

Not in the presence of the boys, he let the twins in on a contribution he had made to their vocabularies.

His last duty performed before leaving Princeton was to initial his piece on a language problem. Not until this decade of Berkeley and Vietnam did the language admit that it hadn't provided a satisfactory word for the arrangement Lois and he had in their youth when they glossed and stammered *living together . . . lovers . . . shacking up . . .* The new era ventured *lovers* again . . . *friends* ("friends!" Maxine jeered) . . . *MH* ("Man of the House!" Maxine jeered. "And what is she—Lady

in Waiting?") Jill explained, "Not man *of*, Mother, man *in*" . . .
Companion . . . Relationship . . . Live-in . . .

"*—as though*," he observed on his sacred bimonthly page,
irretrievably released to the printer, "*the phenomenon were
known only by an untranslatable Yiddishism. There hasn't been a
comparable dilemma since Vitaphone — Talkies — Sound Movies. We
fell back comfortably to plain old movies until film entered in the
dark while nobody was looking, seated herself and took our hand. We
found her attractive. Language decides, and we can only accede.*"

He told his nieces who now lived in this nameless mode the
word he had offered.

"Consort."

The glance exchanged told him he may have begun to pass
beyond his own time. Either that, or the new generation was
in possession of ground it did not have the vocabulary to
hold. Worse yet, vocabulary was becoming irrelevant. He
wished he hadn't released the copy without a field test.

He told them about his years at Columbia, exaggerating
episodes that anticipated current radical styles — reefer parties
with jazzmen, hanging out in the Morningside woods with
bottles of high-test homemade wine. He had heard about
most of it rather than done it. He had no genetic inclination
toward alcohol or reefers, and the style had not been set by
his parents who smoked nothing and tasted alcohol only to
wet their lips with ceremonial port. Rossberger and Riordan
and Letkau lurking on the edge of the English Department
with their impossible poems, the worst poems ever written in
the English language, mocking everything with their eyes,
were not companions in vice — all they were good for was
some good bull about Rimbaud and Mallarmé.

"Martin Letkau was a classmate of mine. We had another
poet in our class, Kinthall Riordan who lived in the Bronx and
went home every night. Riordan's mother fermented a wine
from oranges. I suppose it wasn't fit to drink but I didn't
know any better. We had kind of a den on the heights where
we could put our backs to a stone boulder and be alone to
drink and read our poems. I heard Letkau's poetry before the

New Yorker published it, before he won a Pulitzer." He had done that once. Letkau had read a poem.

They had never heard of Martin Letkau. They knew a poet from Columbia, Ginsberg. When Lloyd had first heard about Ginsberg he had been prepared to think he was a joke. He had read "Howl" in order to keep in touch and had been shaken.

"He is authentic," he assured them. "Ginsberg is an extraordinary poet and may be a great one. He shows no signs of mastering the shorter historic forms, but neither did Whitman."

They had never read Ginsberg. They had heard him read and play finger cymbals.

No discussion that gave him an idea was wasted. "We are going to do a piece on Ginsberg. I might do it myself if I find the time. Shall we call it a day? I will sit on the porch for awhile. The bathroom is yours."

He saw them into their sleeping bags and stumped across the dune to arrange with Mrs Hooter to come by in the morning and warn him that camping was a violation. Sorry.

In the morning he got them parking space at a guest house in Provincetown. He told the keeper to hold the bill for him, as long as they wanted to stay. They were family. He urged them to get on the phone and check in with Maxine, let her know where they were. She cared. They talked about loving trees and animals and Vietnamese, resonances heard by those for whom a few words must go a long way, language creating categories. It was supposed to be the other way around. Their mother loved them with the emotion for which the word had been invented and for which it should be reserved. She would want to know they were okay.

He hadn't known he could speak so eloquently of familial love. Get on that phone! The Cro-Magnon and Robespierre looked at him making the speech as if he were a headless chicken; he returned the look as though they were the ones who bit it off.

They lived out of a Dodge station wagon camouflaged with

petered-out resolutions to peen out dents and abrade rust
down to metal. Panels had got as far as undercoats of chrome
yellow and dried blood. It would be unremarkable at the
Whitney. Boxes filled the bay in front of the tailgate. He told
them to be sure to stop by again before they left to canvass
the south-shore towns with their pots. The wagon lumbered
down the sand road, passed from sight between shoulders of
dune, reappeared on the hardtop and soon passed beyond
that too.

He looked at his watch and saw it would be a good time to
call Ada. The moon lacked two or three days of full. It would
be magnificent running behind the gates of scattered clouds,
looking for ways to get in. Come up for dessert. He had a
piece of chocolate cake—one of those crisp Vienna master-
works. He could offer a spoonful of ice cream for her coffee
but he had only strawberry. She should bring her own cream.
She should bring herself sloppy inside a shift.

As long as he continued to find Gibson #7 habitable and
good for his image, Lois endured it as a good wife for a few
days every summer, then left him to the life he found so
unaccountably agreeable. He performed his act of self-denial,
made confident by experience that having done her annual
duty Lois would not return to these mean quarters. After he
had as much of it as he cared for he would rejoin her as in
other years in Princeton to resume the amenities of their
lives.

Good Works

1

THE ads in the school papers and summer-theater pro-
grams and church-bazaar fliers aren't from stores in the
mall, they're from Henryot's or The Pharm or Beth's or me.
When two high-school girls come in with those big notebooks
(they always travel in pairs to sell ads; it's such a, you know,
like an *awful* experience asking strangers for money) I can tell
it's an ad as soon as they walk in the door.

If it isn't an ad it's raffle tickets or they want merchandise
for an auction. They think we get merchandise free. They talk
about sales and profits as if they were the same. They don't
know anything. They know what I knew at their age.

I always used to ask their names. I used to think, Do I know
her mother? Is her mother a customer? What circulation do I
get? I let them know in a polite way it was blackmail. Before I
gave in I asked why they didn't go to the mall and ask those
big jeans outfits they give all their business to, those mix-and-
match tycoons listed on the stock exchange. I got back the
kind of S.A.T. 850 look that tells the Japanese they're going to
inherit the world. Sometimes they enlightened me, "There's
nobody to talk to at those places. It's a big deal. They have to
get an okay from Oklahoma."

So they nickel-and-dime the local merchants to death.

I was always aggravated by it until Mahlon Weber said,
"Forget it. What does it amount to? Make believe you had to
take a couple hundred dollars a year more in markdowns.
Dole it out with a big smile as if you enjoyed it. They'll tell
their mothers how nice you are."

Fair enough. Mahlon was a real-estate man but he knew

more about stores than anybody else. When my husband was killed in the head-on on that damn Route 6 and I had the insurance money, I thought of opening a shop and asked Mahlon for a location. I mentioned the new strip of shops they were building in back of the printing plant.

"Forget it. Not one of those people will be in business in five years. They can't make a *living* in rooms that small, Eleanor, only jewelers can make a living in three hundred square feet on Cape Cod except in a mall. Work for somebody for a year and find out some things. Then come and see me if you still want to do it." And I did.

That was eighteen years ago. I still don't do anything important without first having coffee with Mahlon Weber.

It was my first year in business and I was still in my grudging mode about ads when a frail little black man wearing a clerical collar came in. I knew as soon as he walked in the door he wanted some kind of contribution and I knew I not only was going to give it to him but I wanted to. I was on his side. We didn't see many black people shopping gift stores at my end of the Cape. We see more now, mostly professionals—lawyers and doctors who know their way around. Portuguese people are part of the scene here like everybody else, but that's not black. A few resort areas on the Vineyard and around Bass River and Hyannis have substantial black clientele. They just don't come to this part of the Cape, or they hurdle it and go to Provincetown. I don't know the details. I don't try to save the world. I just open my door.

I can't tell you how simpatico I felt for this little guy before he even opened his mouth. It was as hot an afternoon in August as we ever get. Everybody was at the beach, we had only a couple of elderly non-swimmers poking through the stock, and here comes this little ancestrally black preacher in a big collar he could have entered from the bottom, a Capone-brim black felt hat, winter-weight black suit, black shirt, black police shoes. No gloves? He took off the hat and wiped the sweatband and his face. He excavated sweat inside the collar with a handkerchief that had been folded and padded more than once looking for a dry corner. He wiped the top of his head. He had fine small features and amused eyes. He was I thought quite old but I really couldn't tell as he had no hair to give me a clue. In retrospect, he was probably a well-worn sixty.

"How would you like a Coke?" I offered. I kept a few things with my lunch in a refrigerator in the stockroom. "I never saw anybody who needed it more."

"Oh thank you very much." His voice was breathy and barely audible. His head stuck out of his collar like a head at a carnival to throw a ball at. He screwed up his face to a smile, pure, sweet and guileless. "Could I have a glass of cold water? That would be fine."

"You're welcome to a Coke."

"Thank you very much. A glass of cold water would be fine."

I asked him to sit down while I filled his order and he was glad to be off his feet. He disposed of the water with evident pleasure, saving an inch for later.

"I'm Eleanor MacAlly. It's my store. What can I do for you?"

He had an envelope of credentials and offered each in turn as he spoke: a worn business card with his photograph and the imprint of The Lord's Will Church, the last card, shown for identification only and put back in the envelope; a letter that had been folded many times, the creases split; a small spiral notebook in which names had been penciled by a patient, unskilled hand.

"I am Reverend Hesterson of The Lord's Will Church—"

"Which is where?"

It broke the trend of his presentation. He regrouped. "We are in Wuster. I move to Hyannis in the summer to do the Lord's work. I came to see if you would help us keep our children in the camp. We bring boys from the city to the outdoors. They so appreciate it. We have many friends who help us with contributions. The folks are good to us. Do you know Mr Seymour Larrick?" He didn't seem to have enough breath to say all that, but by replenishing as he went along he managed.

Mr Larrick's torn letter testified that Reverend Zeal Hesterson was well known to the writer and that he did many good works. Mr Larrick's letter was from five years before. His address was Providence. My impulse was to go into that. I decided not to pry.

Hesterson opened his lined, worn notebook toward me. On each line was a name and an amount. The amounts were mostly one or two dollars. There were fives, very few tens, and a saintly twenty-five. I recognized only a few names. Lou Potch, the oil dealer, president of the Merchant's Association, was down for two dollars. Beth Hannon who had the Killarney shop was down for five. I wanted to weep for the artlessness of a solicitation that allowed me to be heroic for five dollars. He took a receipt pad from his pocket and acknowledged my contribution.

"The children will bless you," he assured me.

I said I wished it could be more but this was a new business. He said the Lord would bless me. I said I could use the help.

Hesterson passed from my mind until the following August, on a rainy day. The store was flooded with customers. I had my head down at the counter writing a sale and glimpsed him standing quietly aside, under the overhanging black hat. To seal in the steam, a black military raincoat— much oversize—sagged from his shoulders to his knuckles and on toward his ankles. I didn't know how long he had been there. He had done nothing to catch my attention. I motioned him toward the office and got to him as soon as there was a break. The few seconds I could give him were enough to tell him where to get a glass of water and do anything else he had to do after walking around all day. I raised him to seven dollars.

He came in every year. He showed me pictures of his boys—four of them bunched on a porch swing, another several with their arms around each other buddy-style. One year a woman—also in black from head to toe with the credentials in a big black patent handbag—introduced herself as Sister Marie. Reverend Hesterson wasn't feeling too good and she was doing his rounds. I sent him my best wishes and the ten that had by then become my amount. He survived his indisposition and was back on the beat the next year.

"I'm going to give you fifteen dollars," I said. "Put it in the book for ten. I don't want to stick my head up."

"That is so fine of you. The Lord will bless you."

"You took care of that already."

At a dinner meeting of the Merchants somebody said we ought to do something about all these solicitations. We should have a common front. Of course nobody knew what to do, it was just self-expression. I spoke up. "Whatever you do, don't do anything to hurt my friend the Reverend Zeal Hesterson. He does great work. I recommended him to you all."

Not many merchants knew what reverend I was talking about until I identified him as the little black preacher. Then everybody knew him. They traded information around the room. He had been coming ten years—no, it was more like twelve. He wasn't in Hyannis, he was in Centerville. On a pond in Marstons Mills. He wasn't local. We were South Westham merchants, we had enough to do taking care of our own. Well, people could do what they wanted. We passed a motion for the secretary to send a letter to the manager of the mall calling on him to urge all his merchants to support local activities. "Mark on the envelope 'Throw Directly in Waste Basket,'" mumbled Grove Lanpheer.

"They can do what they want with it," the secretary said. "It will make a story in the papers that we asked for support for local activities."

After the meeting, the question occurred to me for the first time: what are the logistics of Hesterson's fund-raising? Why is he all the way down here in South Westham? How does he decide who gets the privilege of a solicitation?

I stopped in to have the motel's continental breakfast with friends staying at Ship Wright's where Center Street comes into town off Route 6. The morning sun hadn't yet come up to speed. We sat on the porch settling world affairs and watching the amazing amount of traffic coming into town that early, a stream of vacationers getting shopping and laundry out of the way so they could go to the beach, a lot of vans and pickups with local workmen headed for jobs; and the Reverend Zeal Hesterson and Sister Marie, parking in the small empty lot next to that important-looking electrical setup; generators or dynamos—a rig of the electric company. Nobody thinks to park there, but it doesn't say *No Parking* and there is shade all day long.

Sister Marie went into the foreign-car agency on the corner. Hesterson crossed the street and went into the bank. I was still telling my friends about Hesterson, when he came out and went into the oculist's shop next door. In a minute or two Sister Marie finished at the car agency and went next-door to Anthony's Letter Shop. I didn't see them when I drove through town to my store. When I came back to the center for lunch I saw him going into the toy store.

He got to me at the usual time, mid-afternoon. We talked about the logistics. He and Sister Marie began on the main street at one end of every town on Cape Cod from Falmouth to Provincetown and went on to the end of the day. Then they walked back and got their car. In some towns like ours they did more than one street, some towns took two or three days, some like Truro they could do in a morning. All summer, rain or shine, door to door, wearing their credentials of respectability.

"That's some schedule," I said.

"The Lord has in mind to ask no more than we can give."

"It doesn't allow you much time for the boys, does it?"

"I have good helpers."

I gave him twenty-five. "Show me on the list for ten, same as before."

He thanked me and got up to leave. I noticed that the tops

of his shoes were wrinkled and slits showed between the uppers and the soles when he walked. He didn't walk easily. He walked as if he didn't want to roll over on his toes. He walked as if his feet hurt. "Get yourself a pair of shoes sometimes." I went to the register again. "This isn't for the camp. This is for shoes."

He gave me his beatific smile. I said, "Remember, that's for you, nobody else. I want to see you in real shoes the next time."

I didn't exact a promise. The next year he showed me that he had new shoes. *Different* shoes, I would have said. They had a European look, narrowing to an acute point after the breadth at the ball. They had no toe cap or pattern. I could see his toes flex under the soft uppers. He probably picked them up at the Goodwill or a Thrift Shop. I bit my tongue and didn't say anything.

In addition to Hesterson, two or three other deserving mendicants were on my summer list. The Cookie Lady came in with packages of marvelous cookies, sugared molasses, oatmeal, fruit hermits. No matter how busy we were I stopped the store and made an announcement. "Friends, this lady sells the most delicious homemade cookies. The proceeds are for a good cause, the Mabel Delcourter House for unfortunate young women in Boston. I recommend her to you."

I broke open a package for customers to sample and the Cookie Lady went around the store selling out of a big wicker basket. The cookies were as good as I said, although on the expensive side. I always took a half dozen packages and doled them out to myself from the freezer, even when I was on a diet. My salespeople took one or two packages, and a few customers always tried them. A leaflet in each package explained that the Mabel Delcourter House gave unfortunate young women a good Christian outlook. It seems to be a characteristic of sacrificial people to print everything in light blue ink. The one card Hesterson showed and put back in the envelope was in light blue ink too.

Another on my list was a guitar player who put on an entertainment in our parking lot every year right after the Fourth of July for (his blue card said) Something Wildlife. The guitar player and the Cookie Lady and the Reverend Zeal Hesterson were my regulars for a few dollars. If I was going to be out of the store around the time they were expected I left word they were to be taken care of the same as if I were there. They had enough walking around to do without coming back if they missed me.

I don't want to give the impression that I feel superior to two-dollar and no-dollar people. People look at things their own way, and somebody I don't see on a list may be taking care of two grandmothers. I do like a good cookie, and I was brought up to be uncomfortable if I don't tithe. Real tithing is before tax. I'm not as good as the way I was brought up, I'm an after-tax person. At rock bottom I'm a no-tax person. I paid Hesterson and the others out of the cash register and charged it to shortage on the day's tally. I don't think that's the way the Internal Revenue Service likes transactions like that handled, but it was easier for me and works out the same for the government, and I didn't want to set up any of my beneficiaries for an IRS letter by showing their names in my expense ledger.

I see that some billion-dollar companies do everything the IRS way and don't pay any taxes at all. They tithe to tax lawyers. The IRS is comfortable with that. You can make up your own mind which cases are the most deserving.

2

For only the second time I can remember, Sister Marie came in at the usual time three or four years ago and said the reverend was peaked. When he felt better he might make a special trip to see some of his good friends, maybe in September. I sent my best wishes and a contribution.

Within a few days, a minor crisis came up and I had to be in Hyannis, a horrendous fate in the summer. We had an artist there who painted scenes on tiles and I needed to see with my own eyes how she was doing on a big order we had for a kitchen wall. I arranged to meet her early to beat the traffic and be back in the shop by ten. You can never quite beat the traffic in summer because there are more people beating the traffic than there is traffic. My session with the tile-painter ran long, and before I was ready to drive back to South Westham it was already late morning.

I thought, while I'm here why not drop in on Hesterson? We had been friends for years and I had never visited the camp. The way things were going I would never visit it, as summer was when I had no time to spare and didn't get on the highway unless I had to, and after Labor Day the camp was gone. I phoned the store to be sure the morning flurry of customers was tapering off and told them I would be back later in the afternoon when everybody was coming off the beach. I had a free day.

The phone book didn't have his name. I hadn't expected it to. I looked up The Church of the Lord's Will under all possible variants and didn't find it. I didn't see anything in the Camps listing. Around the corner at the Chamber of Commerce Hesterson was known but no more than as somebody who had been seen and about whom merchants had made inquiries. I began to feel a challenge.

I asked several merchants who had been established for a long time on Main Street and would have been solicited. They all knew the little black preacher with the collar or Sister Marie but didn't know where they lived or where the camp was. Had I tried the post office?

The post office keeps information close to its vest because you may be a bill collector, but if you ask for something reasonable like the location of a store you get an obliging answer. I asked for the camp. The clerk didn't know but he threw the question in the air, "Wilbur! The old black reverend who has a box? You know? The one who wears the collar? You know anything about a camp he has? Where it is?"

He heard an answer I didn't and passed it to me. "We don't

know about the camp. You can find him on Rascher's Lane. Take 28 west. Watch for Lester Street about a half mile after the rotary. Take a right. Go in to the second left. It's dirt. That's Rascher's. It's only a block or two long and dead ends. He's in there."

My station wagon was in the lot behind the row of stores across the street. I stood between parked cars waiting for a break in three lanes of traffic to coincide, but when it occurred I didn't dart through in the entrepreneurial way that my son warned me would one day put me in the hospital. A feeling that I had left something undone held me back. Was it that— instead of being a pleasant surprise to Hesterson—I might be intruding? Ought I to have let him know with more than "I'll drop in on you someday" said the year before last?

Standing in indecision I realized that I had neglected an obvious source of information. Who would have a better line on a children's camp than the Board of Health? The rule is "When in doubt delay," and a delay to seek knowledge is especially praiseworthy. Town offices were in the adjoining building.

Bureaucrats may take long coffee breaks, they may disappear early Friday afternoon, they may be set in concrete; but the blessed thing about them is that they know. If you want to know something don't ask the president of the United States or a selectman, ask whoever has been in that department since Day One. The firmly-made woman doubtless had. She nodded before I told her all I already knew.

"We hear about that camp. Wherever it is isn't in this county. I know it isn't in my town. I got curious and asked the towns around. It isn't in any town from Harwich to Falmouth."

"The Reverend Mr Hesterson is on Rascher's Lane, that's right, isn't it?"

"He's there with his sister. He rents a four-room house on a quarter-acre. It abuts watershed land. There's no camp in there."

Others might have begun to smell fraud sooner, but they

had not had Zeal Hesterson's lovely smile laid on them, or known that, rain or shine, he walked the length of August days in black sweat-sodden clothes, in shoes with open seams, and preferred a glass of cold water. What crime would such a man commit? Did he keep a chorus girl? Did he bet on horses? I sat in my car deciding whether to go the ten minutes to Rascher's Lane or mind my own business and get back to my shop. I decided I did not wish to pry.

Still, there is something in us that wants it known that we have not been hoodwinked.

3

A real-estate man came in with an offer for the lot that adjoins the store. I called Mahlon Weber to try it out on him. Mahlon was in his eighties. I always thought of him as a man whose mind would slow down but would retain essential clarity, the way we envision age for sound people.

We had not been together for more than a few words for nearly a year, since he and his wife had gone to Florida for their six-months-and-a-day tax year and returned to the Cape. The interval was long enough to isolate a subtle change. He sat erectly as if slightly distrusting the security of the chair. His hand wavered with the cup. I hadn't noticed that before. His responses required more than the expected amount of time to compose and were delivered with a slight rush as if they had been held phrase-by-phrase in a computer's buffer. He didn't encourage me to sell Cape Cod property before I had to, and then "—not at any price that doesn't net you after tax—the fair-market value of the property— before tax. Somebody will be smart enough—to want it that much." The advice couldn't have been better; it was what I thought.

He observed that I studied his lips, waiting for the phrases to fall.

"I'm getting a little rocky. I have a touch of Alzheimer's, Eleanor. I've known it for two years."

"If you do have it, it's the barest trace. You're going to make it all right, Mahlon."

"If I die soon enough. How many years do I have on you? I'm eighty-four."

"Twenty-two. I'm getting there. You're in good shape."

"Save your money, Eleanor. Old age can be expensive. I'm going to pay my own way—all the way—no matter what."

"You did it right."

"I'm lucky. I had an education. I could borrow money to go into business. People came to Cape Cod. For houses. For stores."

"Some people have the same luck and don't use it."

"True, Eleanor. True. You and I used our luck. Most people have no luck to use."

I told him about the Reverend Zeal Hesterson. I told him I had sat in the parking lot, making up my mind what to do; and then driving to Rascher's Lane, which surprised Mahlon as much as it had me after I had, I thought, decided to leave it alone.

"Did you want to have it out with him?"

"I don't know what I wanted. I wanted at least to see what there was to see with my own eyes. I wanted to know. I seem to have been born wanting to know."

I described the neglected street of two short blocks with minimal frame houses on either side and a woods at the end.

"I went to the end of the first block and stopped. There wasn't a soul around. I asked myself what I was doing there. What satisfaction would I have from walking in on him and saying, 'Aha!'? I didn't know if he had ever noticed the station wagon in my lot with the store's card taped to the window. He might be sitting on his porch. I was afraid he might see me. I turned around in a hurry and got out of there."

"Forget it. You did the right thing. People who have no luck—have to be excused some things."

When Mahlon got up to leave, he tested his balance before his first step. He then went on as confidently as a man twenty years younger whose luck might last a few more years.

The following August, in the expected week, Zeal Hesterson appeared, wiping the leather of his hat, on an oppressive overcast day a merchant is entitled to after a week of nothing but that damn sunshine. Our customers appreciate a day off from the beach too. They like a day in the shops—especially mine—before they go home to Worcester, Syracuse, Cleveland, Des Moines. Where else are they going to find Vicki of Pátzcuaro's embroidered Mexican robes and Andersen's Danish pewter and Rose Fox's antique jewelry from New York? The other shops have Cape Cod gifte shoppe stuffe.

The Reverend Hesterson found me in what was building up to be the busiest day of the year. Fortunately we were staffed for it, and I wasn't tied down writing sales. My eye was available for customers who needed a word of information. I greeted customers who were pleased to be recognized after having been in only once before, two years ago. That's the kind of store I have.

I gave Hesterson the keys to the city. After refreshing himself he came to stand beside me in the pottery room, out of the way of the heaviest traffic. I asked him what kind of year it was for the camp.

"It is always a good summer for the boys. It is so different from the city. Is your business successful this year? You have so many customers."

"About as expected. How many boys do you get?"

He ran the numbers in his head. "By the end, more than sixty-five been there. A lot of cars in your parking lot."

I felt welling up a compulsion to go to the edge, to let him suspect that I knew his secret—or might soon come to know it—was *capable* of knowing it if I chose. "That means that for each one- or two-week period you get—how many boys? Eight or ten?"

"It depends. Some stay longer, some not as long."

"Eight or ten at a time?"

"Something like that. Yes, sometimes twelve."

"I'm coming to visit one of these years if you don't mind."

"I would be happy. One day I saw a station wagon like

yours near my house. I thought, our friend Mrs McAlly is coming to visit us. I was disappointed. Next time."

His face wore its usual innocence, but knowing what I thought I knew, I saw in it the capability of guile. Of course. How could he have a survived without guile?

"Someday," I said, and no more. I did not know which of us knew more than the other, more than either or us wanted to know. I didn't want to encourage myself to go further.

He took out the same old notebook—or one worn exactly like it. Pages had lost their grip on the wire binding. He licked two leathery fingers and raised the page with my name and amount penciled in the round childish hand. "You have been good to us. Folks see your name. They give us something because they know you."

All right, then—maybe the camp wasn't in Hyannis. Maybe it wasn't in the county. Maybe it was in the Berkshires or in Maine. Maybe he raised money this way and sent them a check.

What difference did it make if it wasn't anywhere?

If the Lord didn't think Hesterson should have the money He shouldn't have sent him in to see me on a day like that in the suit, the hard collar, the hat, the shoes anybody else would have thrown away. The Lord should have had him mail me a brochure printed in blue ink, so I could give it thought and exercise judgment. If I thought he had something good going I would put him on my list to get a check. There would be a paper trail, the IRS would be happy.

I took two twenties and a ten out of the register and wrote a memo on the tally *$50 Hesterson* to remind myself that the shortage was not accountable to one of the summer girls. "I'm relying on you to do good work. You can show in the book that I gave fifty. Maybe somebody else will be inspired."

He laid his benedictory smile on me. "The Lord will bless you."

I thought perhaps not. The Lord knew what fifty dollars amounted to from somebody born lucky. "If He pleases," I said. "Take care of yourself."

Under the leather his toes flexed, trying to help his hand write my name and *$50*. He folded the ledger and returned it to his breast pocket. "The Lord takes care. He puts us in the way of peril to show He is the One who snatches us back to a safe place."

I thought it roundabout, not the way I would choose; a show-off tithe He would not especially appreciate if I did it. I said I would try to stop by when the boys were there, but it was not easy to get away from the store in the summer.

About the Author

Elliott Stanley Goldman was born in 1913 and grew up in Pittsburgh. He attended the Experimental College of the University of Wisconsin, and the University of Pittsburgh, where he majored in philosophy. In World War II he captained the first U.S. naval vessel—a minesweeper—to have an all-black crew. He began to write fiction in the mid-eighties, after retiring from a successful business career. His stories appear frequently in the *Atlantic*, and his first novel, *Big Chocolate Cookies*, was published in 1988. *Earthly Justice*, winner of the first annual William Goyen Prize for Fiction, is also Mr. Goldman's first story collection. He currently lives on Cape Cod with his wife, the artist Virginia H. Goldman, and is at work on a two-novel saga spanning one hundred years of a Pittsburgh family.

The William Goyen Prize for Fiction

William Goyen was born in 1915 in Trinity, Texas, and died in 1983 in Los Angeles. In his novels and short stories (most notably, *The House of Breath, Arcadio* and *Had I a Hundred Mouths*), he created an extraordinary stylistic originality, he succeeded in an enduring experiment in fictional form and he offered his readers an uncommon range of feeling and insight. Almost all of his work arises from the landscape and characters that he mythicized out of his native east Texas. His fiction is rhapsodic, deeply compassionate and visionary, and everywhere is informed by a sense of life that is sensitive to the eccentricity and oddity of ordinary life, to the vitality of the erotic and the sensual, and to the power of both passion and grief. Known for his generosity to younger writers, he is memorialized with the William Goyen Prize for Fiction, which, in his spirit, is intended to bring recognition to newer or lesser-known writers. The prize includes a $3,000 award and publication royalties.